Monsters & Reapers & Ghosts, Oh My!

Short Story Collection

Judy Lunsford

Monsters & Reapers & Ghosts, Oh My!

Short Story Collection

Judy Lunsford

Introduction

This short story collection is filled with stories written about monsters, ghosts, and all sorts of other creepy creatures. Also included at the very end is The Wild Hunt trilogy in its entirety with all of its monsters and hunters.

Included in this collection are flash fiction stories as well as much longer stories.

Some of the stories in here end well, and others end a little more tragically. I don't know that there is anything truly frightening or horrific here, but for those of you who are familiar with my other work, this volume is not necessarily for younger readers. I tend to shy away from blood and gore in my writing, but some of the imagery may be too intense for very young or sensitive readers.

I hope you find something you like.
Happy reading!

Judy Lunsford
January 2022

We'll kick things off with a short story that received an Honorable Mention in the First Quarter of the 2021 Writer's of the Future contest.

It was a great honor to be chosen by the keeper of the burnings. It was also a terrible responsibility. If the keeper failed, the whole tribe could come to a bloody end at the claws of the creatures. Amka had only been an apprentice for a few days, but soon she would have more to deal with than an apprentice should ever face. Can Amka survive the first days of her apprenticeship? Or will the whole village die with her? Find out how Amka faces the darkness in this chilling story.

The Burning

It was a great honor to be chosen by the keeper of the burnings. It was also a terrible responsibility. If the keeper failed at his job, it could mean the end for the tribe.

Amka had been an apprentice for only a few days, but she was catching on quickly. She never wanted to be chosen, but now that she had, she enjoyed the looks of admiration from the tribe. From the other children. The bullies didn't dare even speak to her now.

Amka's mother had forced her to line up with the other children on the day of the choosing. She hadn't even wanted to leave the house that morning. It was especially cold and it was so warm and cozy under her favorite bear skin blankets. The faint smell of smoke and bear shank cooking for breakfast pleasantly greeted her first waking moments.

Her mother had pulled the warm blankets off of Amka and left her exposed to the cold that had permeated the hut through the night. She had gently pulled Amka to her feet and walked her over to where she had laid out Amka's clothes in front of the fire.

Her mother expected her to line up with the other children, now that she was of age. From the moment she turned twelve, her mother expected her to be chosen. She was the only one who had ever had any faith in Amka. Even her father didn't think Amka would be chosen. He was still asleep, snoring loudly in the next room.

Amka pulled on her clothes and bundled up as warm as she could. She was grateful that her mother had warmed her clothes by the fire before waking her. Her new boots waited for her by the hearth. Before Amka left, her mother smiled at her and kissed her forehead. She spoke traditional words of luck and blessings and hugged Amka before practically pushing her out the door and out into the shocking cold.

No parents were allowed at the choosing. Only the candidates, the chief, and the keeper.

Amka trudged out into the snow. It crunched under her feet as her new boots broke through the surface of the crisp white and crunched down through to Amka's knees. She hated when the snow got to the top of her boots. And this pair was too large and the cold wet started to seep down the tops of her boots, making her shins cold.

Deep snow also meant when the bullies shoved her down, she would not be able to see them again until after she got up. Losing sight of a bully meant additional surprise attacks, which was something Amka hated.

The sky was shimmering with greens and purples as the morning sunlight barely peeked over the jagged pointy tops of the pine trees in the distance. Amka looked out over the huge empty vastness that separated her village from the thick line of trees.

The only thing in the stark white emptiness were thousands upon thousands of small lanterns, all covered with a special tarp that only the keeper knew how to make. The tarp kept the wind and snow from extinguishing the lanterns.

It was the keeper's job to make sure that all of the lanterns stayed lit at night and remained in good repair. And it was the apprentice's job to learn the secrets to keeping them burning. As well as the secrets to keep them from getting buried in snow through the night.

It was the keeper's job to keep the creatures at bay.

The last apprentice had been careless. The creatures had gotten hold of him. It was a common end for an apprentice. A new one was necessary.

Amka walked over to line up with all the other children in front of the chief and the keeper.

Tonraq, one of the boys who constantly bullied her, tripped her so that she fell face-first into the cold white, right in front of the chief and keeper.

All eyes were on her as she slowly got to her feet, her face stinging from the frigid slap to her face. She couldn't bring herself to look at the chief or the keeper. She was too ashamed to meet their gaze after such an embarrassing moment. The other children were laughing and their laughter echoed in the morning emptiness.

The chief ordered the children to be silent. But Amka was still too embarrassed to look up. It was all she could do to not cry. Her nose ran uncontrollably and she sniffed and wiped her nose with her sleeve, trying to keep her back to the other children. She couldn't imagine explaining to her mother what had happened. It would break her heart. The disappointment of Amka not being chosen would be too much.

The keeper walked over and stood in front of Amka. She stared at the tops of his boots. They fit him perfectly. There was no gap to let the snow trickle down to wet his shins. She found herself wondering if he had ever fallen face first into the snow. Or if he had a boy like Tonraq bully him when he was little.

She slowly lifted her eyes to the keeper to see if she could see any clue in his eyes as to whether or not he had been bullied, or if he had been the bully.

When she finally met his gaze, she saw a softness to his eyes. She could never imagine those soft brown eyes to belong to those of a bully. But she couldn't imagine anyone ever picking on him either.

He reached down to her and put his hand out, palm up. In his hand was the amulet of the apprentice. There was a large gouge out of one side with teeth marks punctured almost all the way through it.

He had gotten it back from the creatures. The amulet of the apprentice had survived the attack, even if the boy didn't.

Amka tentatively reached her hand towards the amulet. She had hoped this wasn't a cruel joke. She fully expected him to close his hand around the amulet and snatch it away from her at the last moment. But before she touched it, she looked up at his eyes once again.

There was no malice. No trickery.

She gently picked the amulet up, out of his hand, and stood in front of him holding the prize that all of the other children had wanted.

He smiled at her and then nodded to the chief.

The chief immediately gave the order for all of the other children to go home.

The apprentice had been chosen. And it was Amka.

She was so excited; she couldn't wait to go home and tell her mother. But she knew she wouldn't get the opportunity any time soon. Her mother would know the results before she arrived with the news. The other children filed back into the village to their homes.

Her mother would be waiting with her father on the front porch of their little hut. They would watch children around them go into their homes for breakfast. But Amka wouldn't be among them.

Her mother would be so happy. Her father would be shocked. But Amka would see neither reaction.

On the day of the choosing, the chosen one goes with the keeper to immediately start their training. Not home.

*

Out of all of the children of her tribe, Panuk had chosen Amka to be his apprentice. Days later, Amka was still reeling from the choice. She had to run to keep up with Panuk's long strides in the snow as her short legs and too large boots and wet shins slowed her down during her lessons.

Panuk hadn't spoken to her about why he chose her. But he did give her instructions about what he needed her to do. They worked day and night, sleeping only when the work was done in the daylight.

At night, it was their busiest time. In the darkness, they tended the lanterns that divided the forest from the village.

Amka hated the nights. The darkness was vast and complete. The only light came from the lanterns. A small circle of light emanated around each one. She looked out across the lanterns at the tree line and watched for any movement. She had yet to see a creature.

She hoped against hope that she never would see one, but she knew that as the keeper's apprentice, it was inevitable. She would see one. The question was, would she survive it?

There was no moon. The sky was lit only by the stars and the purples and greens that shimmered above them all of the time. Amka was distracted by the tiny pinholes of light that were scattered in the sky like spilled rice.

Panuk nudged her and brought her focus back to the lantern they were repairing. Amka was grateful that he was gentle with her.

She had seen Panuk yelling at the last apprentice. When she asked him about it, Panuk told her his story.

His constant disobedience and arrogance were what got him killed. He didn't think he needed instruction, so he had ignored Panuk. He wandered too close to the tree line. He had wanted to see a creature. It was the last thing he ever saw.

Panuk had reassured her that there would be no yelling if she obeyed his every instruction. Safety was his main concern. For her and for the tribe.

Amka brought her attention back to the lantern. It was simply out of oil. It had been her job during the day to make sure all of them were filled and ready for the night.

Panuk reminded her that it was easy to miss a lantern during the day's rounds. He quietly reassured her that, in time, she would develop a pattern among them, so that none would get missed in the future.

He kept his voice soft and low in the darkness. Sound travelled across the vast white very easily. He did not want to draw the attention of the creatures.

When the lantern was filled and back to proper burning height, they covered it with the snow shade and stood up.

Panuk scanned the lanterns, looking to see if Amka had missed any others.

Amka saw it before Panuk. She lifted her arm and pointed to one of the farthest lanterns. It was almost to the tree line. And it wasn't lit.

Panuk sighed and looked down at Amka.

"You carry the supplies," he said. "Stay close."

Amka picked up their bag and slung it over her shoulder. The weight of it almost yanked her off her feet. She staggered two steps to the right and almost knocked over another lantern. She quickly regained her balance and ran to catch up with Panuk, who was already several of his long strides ahead of her.

She caught up to him and fell in line behind him. She could feel her breathing grow heavy and labored. Her shins were wet and frost was forming at the tops of her boots.

Panuk stopped walking and put his hand out to indicate that Amka should be silent. He scanned the tree line and stood frozen in place for a long moment.

Amka tried to calm her breathing. It was so loud in her ears that she could swear that the creatures could hear her breathing. She tucked her face sideways and pulled on the lining of her hood with her free hand. She breathed the warm humid air inside of her coat. She wanted to muffle her breathing so that the creatures wouldn't find them.

Panuk looked back at her and saw her with her hood stretched over her face to muffle her mouth. She grinned and shook his head, and then signaled for her to follow him again.

Amka let go of her hood and settled it back on her head properly and continued to follow Panuk. As they drew closer to the tree line, she could feel her heart beat louder and faster.

Fear gripped her chest. This was her first time this close to the trees at night. Only yesterday was her first time close to the trees at all.

Some of the children used to dare each other to go to the tree line during the day, when they could escape the eyes of the adults in the village. But Amka had never dared try. The stories of the creatures horrified her to her very core.

Her hands started shaking as they drew close. Her heartbeat in her ears was becoming deafening. Her breathing had become even more labored and Amka couldn't take her eyes off of the trees.

There were dark shadows hidden in the depths of the darkness. The lanterns lit up the edge of the tree line, causing shadows to dance back and forth across the black. She could only see a few feet into the trees, but she knew it was there.

She reached out to Panuk, to warn him.

He was watching the tree line ahead of the dark lantern. Amka was watching the tree line near the lit ones.

The shadows moved and danced unnaturally, not like the flicker of the flames, but like movement in the darkness.

Before Amka could make a sound, she realized that the *it* was a *they*, and they were everywhere.

Panuk had reached the lantern. But it wasn't out of oil. Amka would have been relieved that it wasn't her carelessness, but she was too frightened for relief when she saw that the lantern had been knocked over.

The broken lantern lay in pieces on the snow. The soapstone base smashed to bits.

Amka was too scared to speak, but she pulled on Panuk's sleeve with two weak jerks at his elbow.

He looked down at her and she pointed to the tree line.

"We're safe," Panuk said. "There's nothing there."

"No," Amka shook her head. Her voice was a strained whisper. "There's dozens of them."

Panuk looked back to the tree line. He squinted into the darkness and scanned the trees.

"I see nothing," he said.

Amka grabbed his sleeve once again and pulled him back.

Panuk suddenly sucked in a deep breath and placed his arm in front of Amka, gently pushing her behind him.

"Back up slowly," he said. "Don't trip over any lanterns."

Amka couldn't tear her eyes away from the tree line.

Slowly, the shadows started coming forward, out in front of the trees. When they were close enough for the light of the lanterns to hit them, nothing about them lit up except for their eyes.

An eerie yellow glow reflected back from the eyes of each creature. Amka started counting.

One, two, three, four…

Panuk continued to push her backwards.

Seven, eight, nine…

Amka stepped back slowly, she almost naturally steered around another lantern, and felt the warm glow of its light envelop her as she passed it.

Fifteen, sixteen, seventeen…

Her eyes had only made it halfway across the tree line as she counted.

A bell sounded behind her. Amka had never been so relieved to hear the ear shattering clanging of the tribe's warning bell. The watchers had seen Panuk and Amka backing away from the tree line and were ringing out the battle warning.

The village behind them started to light up and the men from the village were shouting and lighting torches from the fires along the village edge.

Before long, Amka could hear the crunching of footsteps in the snow behind her. There were so many torches coming up from behind her that she could feel the warmth of the fires cut through the icy chill of the night.

The warriors sped past Panuk and Amka and charged the tree line with shouts and fire and steel. Their swords had been dipped in the oil used in the lanterns and they had lit them aflame. Their war cries and their flaming steel were their only weapons against the shadowy creatures of the night.

Amka watched the eyes back away and disappear into the darkness once again.

Panuk grabbed her by the shoulder of her jacket near her hood and pulled her along, returning to the broken lantern. The warriors surrounded them while they hurriedly made a makeshift repair to the lantern. The base was shattered, but they could put a temporary replacement in its stead and it would light up and last until morning.

Amka worked fast, her hands shaking so badly that she almost couldn't be of any use.

Panuk did most of the work, but Amka was able to light the flame and gather their tools back into Panuk's bag.

As soon as they were finished, Panuk grabbed Amka by the arm and pulled her to her feet. He grabbed their bag and swung it effortlessly over his shoulder.

"Come with me," Panuk ordered.

He pulled her along beside him by her arm and she had to run to keep up.

Amka tripped in the deep snow again and again as Panuk pulled her along. His strong grip never let her fall, but her shorter legs wouldn't let her keep up. Panuk practically dragged her back to the village and didn't let go of her until they had passed the blazing war fires and were back to his hut.

Panuk pulled her inside and dropped his bag at the doorway.

Jissika, Panuk's wife, was waiting for them with a blazing fire and hot coffee.

Panuk pulled Amka over to the table by the fire and set her firmly down in a straight-backed chair. She felt off balance and confused. She didn't know what she did wrong, or why Panuk was so angry with her.

"How did you know?" he demanded.

"What happened?" Jissika asked.

Panuk looked directly into Amka's eyes. There was a fire in his eyes that was burning almost as hot as the fire in the stone fireplace behind her.

"How did you know?" he demanded again.

"There were," Amka swallowed. Her mouth was so dry that she couldn't speak. She tried to wet her mouth and tried again. "Shadows."

"What shadows?" Panuk demanded. "There was only darkness."

Amka shook her head. "There were shadows in the dark."

Panuk looked at his hands and realized he was gripping Amka's arms tightly. He released his grip and Amka could feel the blood flow return to her hands.

"She saved my life," Panuk looked over at Jissika.

"How?" his wife asked.

"She could see them," Panuk sat down on another chair and stared at Amka.

Jissika handed each of them a steaming mug of coffee.

Amka took it gratefully and sipped at the hot liquid. Jissika had made Amka's the way she liked it. With lots of sugar. The wetness returned to her mouth and the hot coffee cooled the fire that was choking down her throat. She savored the bittersweet flavor as she started to feel her hands relax from all of the shaking from fear and cold.

Jissika sat down on the other side of the table and quietly waited.

"What did you see, exactly?" Panuk asked.

"Are you angry?" Amka asked timidly.

Panuk exchanged looks with Jissika, who smiled softly at him and shook her head, and then looked back at Amka.

"I'm not angry," Panuk softened his voice. "I was forceful with you because I wanted you to stay safe. If I hurt you, I am truly sorry, but I did what had to be done in the moment."

Amka nodded and held her steaming mug tightly to her chest. She was starting to sweat inside of her coat.

As if reading her mind, Panuk pulled off his own jacket and gloves.

Jissika came over and gently took Amka's mug from her and helped Amka remove her coat and gloves. Amka immediately took the steaming mug back from the table and clutched it to her chest once again.

"I'm not angry," Panuk said softly, facing her knee-to-knee with their chairs. "I just want to know what you saw."

Amka shrugged, "I told you. There were shadows in the dark."

"That doesn't make any sense," Panuk sat back in his chair. "There are no shadows in the pitch black of that forest."

Amka stared at the hot brown liquid in her mug. A small bubble glided across the surface and it drew Amka's attention for a brief moment.

Jessika leaned forward onto the table and reached out for her husband's hand.

Panuk reached back and they interlaced their fingers on top of the table.

Amka watched without lifting her head. Her parents never showed each other the kind of affection she witnessed Panuk and Jissika express towards one another. Hostility ruled her home. But here, Amka felt comfortable.

"There are the legends," Jissika said.

"That's all they are." Panuk shook his head, "Legends."

"What legends?" Amka asked.

"Legends of the true keepers," Jissika said. "The naturals."

Amka looked to Panuk for an explanation.

Panuk shrugged and took a sip of his coffee. "There are legends that there are natural born keepers. They can see the creatures, they learn the trade faster, that sort of thing."

"Why haven't I heard the legend before?" Amka asked.

Panuk shrugged again. "Because there's no such thing. It's just a story."

There was a knock at the door.

Panuk rose and answered. The chief stood in the doorway and gestured for Panuk to step outside.

Jissika rose and handed Panuk his gloves and coat. He took them from her and put them on as he followed the chief outside.

"Should I go with him?" Amka asked, unsure of what she should do at the moment.

Jissika shook her head and sat down in Panuk's chair, facing Amka.

"Listen to me," Jissika said. "A natural could save the village."

"How?" Amka asked.

"A natural keeper can control the burning of the fire," Jissika said, almost in a whisper. "It is a long-forgotten magic, but it's still there."

"Where?" Amka asked.

Jissika pointed at Amka's heart, "I think it's in there."

Amka shook her head, "I don't have any family history of being a keeper. I'm the first."

"It doesn't matter," Jissika said. "It's not in a family line, it's in the keeper's heart. You have the heart of a natural."

"How do you know?" Amka asked.

"You're learning twice as fast as Panuk's best apprentice," Jissika said. "You've learned in days what took weeks and even months for the others."

Amka stared at the bubble that still floated at the top of her coffee.

"But I haven't survived as long," Amka whispered.

"Yet," Jissika smiled. "You saved Panuk tonight. No other apprentice has done that."

Amka shrugged, not knowing what to say.

"You need to learn to focus the magic," Jissika started.

The door flew open and Panuk came back inside. He was alone.

Panuk shut the door and took off his gloves and coat and threw them down to warm by the fire.

"The warriors have things taken care of for the night," Panuk said. "You need sleep. Tarkik is waiting outside to walk you home."

Amka nodded and slid off her chair. Jissika helped her into her coat and gloves and Amka and headed out into the frigid cold to be escorted home by a warrior.

*

Word spread quickly in the village about what had occurred in the darkness the night before. The bullies no longer bullied Amka. In fact, they avoided her altogether.

Amka watched as Tonraq was playing with some other boys in the village. When Tonraq looked up and saw her, he stared at her with fear in his eyes. Before the other boys could notice, he casually suggested that they go play somewhere else.

Amka was left standing alone over a soapstone base with Panuk's tools in her hands. She knelt down on her work tarp and tried not to cry.

She could hear the girls in the village playing nearby. Amka wiped the tears away and continued her work. Panuk wanted more lanterns spread along the tree line before dark. The chief had demanded the front line doubled before nightfall.

Amka focused on her work, trying to drown out the loss of her childhood with her chores. She was to be the next keeper. Playtime was over.

Amka let her thoughts wander to what Jissika had said. There was magic involved with the making of the lanterns, but not much. She stared at the tarps that Panuk made to go over the lanterns. He infused them with magic so that they could withstand wind, snow, and whatever other harsh treatment the elements could throw at them.

Panuk's tarps could withstand a blizzard. She remembered back two winters ago, when there was the worst blizzard their village had seen in decades. Panuk's magic had kept the lanterns burning. And even more amazing, Panuk's magic had kept the lanterns on top of the snow as it piled up from the storm.

The snow had risen several feet over the course of the night, and the lanterns still remained lit and settled into the top of the snow.

Amka knew the keepers used magic. But as she worked, she wondered how much had been forgotten.

Panuk returned with the carcass necessary to make the oil they would use to keep the new lanterns burning and dropped it near Amka. She hated that part of the job. Without a word, she pulled out her knife and set to work.

By the end of the day, Amka and Panuk had set out twice the number of lanterns near the tree line than there was the evening before. It was their first line of defense.

Panuk and the chief were hoping that the extra light would keep the creatures at bay.

Amka watched the tree line while they worked. She saw no sign of the shadows dancing in the darkness. Just pine trees covered in a frosting of white.

When darkness fell, the lanterns were lit and the warriors were working out shifts for taking turns on watch. They didn't want to be caught off guard if the creatures dared to breach the light again.

Panuk and Amka stayed on watch as well. Amka was getting used to the long hours that were put in by a keeper. But it was mostly fear and adrenaline that kept her awake through the long nights.

That night, she felt especially awake in the early part of the evening.

Her eyes scanned the tree line, into the darkness. As the night drew on, there was no sign of the creatures.

Panuk sat by one of the war fires, helping to keep the fire watchers awake through the night. The whole village was lit up, as it would be if the bell had been rung.

Amka was nodding off by the fire several feet away from Panuk. It had been a long day and she felt sleep weighing heavily on her eyelids.

Panuk nudged her and handed her a hot cup of coffee. Amka took it and smiled sheepishly. Panuk grinned and walked back to the fire and the other men.

Amka took a sip of the hot black liquid. There was no sugar. She held the bitterness in her mouth for a moment and then swallowed, letting the heat of the mug warm her hands through her gloves.

Amka looked up across the vast white expanse filled with the yellow glow of the lanterns and into the darkness of the trees. She saw movement.

She stood up quickly, spilling her coffee onto the ground. Amka stared at the tree line intently, searching for shadows.

Panuk made a warning sound and all of the men fell silent.

Panuk walked quietly over to where Amka stood, and stared out to the trees where Amka was watching.

A line of warriors armed with flaming swords came and flanked Panuk and Amka.

"Should we sound the bell?" one of the men asked.

Panuk looked down at Amka, who was slowly walking towards the expanse of lanterns with her eyes fixed on the tree line.

"Sound it," Panuk said behind her.

Moments later, the bell was being rung and the metallic cacophony echoed out over the expanse of yellow glow.

Amka could hear the other warriors rising and running out to fortify the line.

She continued watching the trees and the shadows that were coming forward towards her. Their eyes started to glow in the light of the lanterns. But their bodies remained in shadow, even as they came into the light.

When they reached the front line of light, they each, one at a time, kicked over the lanterns, extinguishing them in the snow.

Warriors ran past Amka in full charge, their screams tearing past her like the gales of a strong winter blizzard. They had their fire and steel at the ready and they hit the tree line already swinging their weapons for battle.

Amka watched in horror as the creatures ripped through the warriors like they were nothing. Bodies of her fellow villagers lay on the snow, their blood seeping red into the stark white.

"Amka, come back," Panuk yelled from somewhere behind her.

Amka could feel the fires behind her flare into the full battle line. A wall of flames used only when the creatures broke the tree line. She had unknowingly crossed the line and was on the wrong side of the fires.

Something pulled her forwards.

Amka locked eyes with one of the creatures. It stepped on the body of Tarkik, the warrior who had escorted her home the night before, and creeped out deeper into the lanterns and their light.

She could hear the screams of her mother behind her, calling for her to come back. It sounded so distant and far away. Muffled like a dream.

Amka ignored the cries and kept moving forwards towards the creature advancing towards her. It was the alpha, and the other shadow creatures were closing in behind him.

Amka didn't take her eyes from the alpha. He was as big as Panuk's hut, and she could see its muscles tighten. Even up close, the creature was hidden in shadow. The light of the lanterns no longer had any affect. The alpha advanced on her and through the shadow of itself, she could see it ready to pounce.

Amka stared the creature in the eyes. She was so close to its face that she could see herself. Her own reflection in the yellow glow of the lantern-lit eyes.

Amka's mother screamed behind her, and Panuk desperately called her name.

She couldn't take her eyes off the creature. She felt hot, like she was standing in a fire herself. Amka started sweating under her coat and felt like her chest was on fire.

The creature suddenly stopped and stared at Amka with fear in its eyes. The type of fear when one realized that it has gone from being the hunter to the hunted.

The creature reeled back, but it was too late.

Amka focused the flames that she felt coursing through her veins and screamed with all her might from the pain. She threw her head back and let the fire out.

The creature in front of her burst into flames. Its screams shattered the silence in the forest and shook the trees.

The other creatures, all the way back to the tree line, exploded into flames and the pine trees that had lost their snow became unrooted and started to fall.

Amka, completely exhausted, fell face first into the snow.

She turned her head and looked into the eyes of the burning creature that lay in the snow in front of her. As her eyes closed, she smiled because she knew the creature was no longer a threat.

*

When she awoke, Amka didn't know where she was at first.

When her eyes came back into focus, she realized that she was in Panuk's hut. Jissika was sitting by her bedside checking a dressing that covered Amka's arm.

"What happened?" Amka asked.

Jissika smiled and leaned towards Amka and stroked her face.

"You're a natural," she whispered. "I knew you had it in you."

"What did I do?" Amka asked.

"You took control of the war fires," Jissika said. "It was amazing. The wall of flames behind you became your weapon. You set all of the creatures on fire and burned them to ash."

"Is it over?" Amka asked. "Are they all gone?"

The smile faded from Jissika's face.

"They're all gone now, right?" Amka was confused. "If I burned them, they're gone, right?"

"Not yet," Jissika whispered.

The door opened and Panuk came into the hut.

"She's awake?" he asked.

"Yes," Jissika looked over her shoulder at Panuk.

He came over and sat down in a chair next to the bed.

Panuk's face was serious as he looked down at Amka.

"Somebody please tell me what happened," Amka demanded.

She tried to sit up, but suddenly found herself in scorching pain. Amka pulled the bandage off of her arm and looked at her injuries for the first time.

She had severe burns going up both arms all the way from her fingertips to her shoulders. The burns followed the lines of her veins and were physically hot to the touch. She looked down and saw the same burns scorched across her chest.

Amka looked up at Jissika, whose eyes were filled with tears.

Amka reached her hands to her face and she could feel the same scarring reaching up her neck to her face.

She started to panic.

"It's okay," Jissika said. "Your burns are healing quickly."

"What?" Amka said. She felt like she couldn't control her breathing. She gasped for air as she tried to make sense of what Jissika said.

"Your burns, they were much worse last night," Jissika said. "You're healing. It must be a result of being a natural."

Amka looked at Panuk. He stared at her like he had never seen her before.

"I'm so sorry I chose you," he said.

Amka felt like she had been shot through the chest by one of the hunter's arrows.

"How could you say that?" she asked.

"You being chosen, it activated your powers," he said. "The creatures are drawn to you, just as you are drawn to them. When I chose you to be my apprentice, I put you in extreme danger."

"But I can end this," Amka said. "We know I can burn them. And I can heal."

Panuk looked at Jissika and then back to Amka.

"It's not that simple," he said.

"Why not?" she asked.

Panuk sighed heavily and looked at Jissika once again.

"She must see it," Jissika said softly.

Panuk stood and started to put on his coat.

"Come with me," he said.

Amka rose from the bed and followed Panuk outside.

Jissika followed behind her carrying Amka's boots and coat.

Amka didn't feel the cold or the snow.

As she walked outside, the snow melted for several feet around her as she walked.

Amka walked on bare ground for the first time in her life as she stepped out of Panuk's hut and walked through the village.

Everyone around her stopped what they were doing as Amka walked past. Children started to cry when they saw her. Even Tonraq stepped away from her in fear.

Amka made her way around Panuk's hut and to the edge of the village, where she could see out across the vast expanse of white that used to lead to the forest.

Instead of the jagged pine trees that lined the edge of the forest, there was nothing but ash. The location of the trees and the creatures were only marked by ash and blackened scorch marks on the ground.

Amka made her way across the expanse. Hundreds of lanterns lay crushed and extinguished in the snow.

Amka ignored the jagged pieces of soapstone that lay scattered around her. The snow melted in front of her and the water steamed up from the baked dry ground beneath her feet.

She carved a path through the expanse and to the tree line. She never once took her eyes off of what lay ahead of her, now exposed to the light of day. The trees of the forest lay on the parched earth, crumbling into ash as she walked past them.

As she made her way into the remains of the forest, she saw what had worried Jissika and Panuk.

A huge cavernous hole stood in the middle of the forest. It was as tall as any tree that would have been hiding it. It looked like the mouth of a cave, except for the fact that there was nothing around it. Just a black hole standing in what was left of the forest.

Amka felt drawn to the opening.

She walked closer to it and examined it from close range. It was nothing but pitch black.

Amka looked back towards the village. A crowd had gathered to watch her. The entire village crowded into the expanse, but remained close to the village. Mothers held their children close. The remaining warriors held their weapons ready and were keeping the war fires burning.

She searched their faces until she saw her parents standing with Panuk and Jissika. They were at the front of the crowd, almost dead center.

Amka turned back to the black hole and reached out to it.

It stood silent, black, still. Until she touched it.

As soon as Amka's fingers touched the black, a shrill scream filled the air. It brought Amka to her knees with her hands covering her ears.

When the shrieking stopped, Amka looked back at the villagers. They had been covering their ears and cowering from the sound as well.

Amka met Jissika's eyes across the expanse.

She remembered Jissika's words.

A natural could save the village.

Amka turned to face the black hole in front of her. She summoned up all of the strength she had left and focused on the hole.

The villagers shrieked behind her as the war fires shot up high into the sky and then came back down to earth. The flames scorched their way across the expanse, drawing more power from each lantern that remained burning as it passed.

Amka focused the power of the flames through the black hole. She could feel herself burning, but remained focused on the vast darkness of the hole.

The war fires shot through into the darkness and carried her with it, through the hole and into the black. She could feel herself dying. The power of the darkness was too much for her on her own.

But suddenly, there was a second surge of power. The flames increased and Amka felt like she was having a second wind. She focused her mind once again and directed the flames into the darkness. When she felt the flames no more, she blacked out and fell to the earth.

All Amka could feel anymore was cold. There was no darkness, only white. And the feeling of being drawn by some inexplicable force was gone.

Amka opened her eyes, expecting to see the shimmering purple and greens of the sky. But instead, she saw her father's face.

He reached his hand out to her to help her to her feet. He wasn't wearing his coat or his gloves.

She looked at his arm and saw the burns that followed the veins up his arm to his shoulder.

Amka stared at her father with amazement, "You?"

Her father nodded. She took his hand and he pulled her to her feet.

Her burns matched his, almost exactly. The signs of a true natural. The burnings that indicated that they had the power to keep the creatures of the darkness at bay.

The creatures would be back. They always found a way. But the next time, the naturals would be ready.

Here's a more light-hearted flash fiction piece.

Howard

I wish that my landlord had told me that there was something very wrong with my apartment before I moved in.

I sometimes wonder if it is just my place, or if it is the whole building. But none of my neighbors are very talkative and always seem rather nervous when I approach them.

At first, it was just small things going missing. A lighter, a spoon I swear I left on the kitchen counter, my spare set of keys. Then larger things started to disappear. My shoes, my tablet, the microwave.

It was frustrating at first, because I just thought I was losing my mind. But then I figured it out.

There's something living in the closet by the front door.

To be honest, the only thing I put in there when I moved in was my vacuum cleaner. And I use it so rarely, it took a little while to figure out that it had gone missing too.

Well, the vacuum cleaner didn't go missing so much as it seems that I gave it to him.

I'm not sure what he is exactly, but he is a dark bluish purple and has more tentacles than I can count. I've only seen him face-to-face once, when I went in to get my vacuum. He scared the crap out of me so bad that I haven't opened the door to that closet since.

But he's in there. I can hear him.

And occasionally, a long tentacle comes out when he cracks the closet door open slightly and peers out at me.

The tentacle is always searching for something.

So I've started giving him things.

He seems to like shiny objects, so that's what I try to give him. I've even found myself buying "presents" for him, to keep him happy.

I just gave him a small mirror that I found at the drug store the other day. He's been in there making happy cooing noises ever since.

I've also taken to feeding him. This was more of a matter of self-defense thinking than anything else. He likes burgers and pizza, so I just order two when I get takeout.

I guess I should be mad at my landlord, but the rent for this place is something I couldn't pass up, even with some sort of leviathan creature living in my closet.

Howard, that's what I named him, and I get along just fine. Delivery guys usually just leave things at the front door. The guy that Howard sent a tentacle out to snatch a pizza from has never been back, but the new pizza guy has gotten used to him and occasionally even asks about Howard.

But no one wants to come inside.

I can't say I blame them.

But I kind of like Howard.

He's a good listener and we've come to a sort of understanding.

He's the best roommate I've ever had.

This one starts with a baby. Don't worry, she's all right.

Murder of Crows

The baby was laying in her crib, just inside the window. The rising sun was peeking through the open frame and illuminating the baby's blanket with the first rays of the morning light.

The baby was crying, unnoticed by her father who was sound asleep in the next room.

The crow flew to the window and landed on the sill and looked into the room at the baby girl as she wailed loudly.

The crow cawed down at the baby and the startled baby looked up, silenced for a brief moment, and stared at the crow that was staring back down at her.

She started to cry once again.

The crow cawed again and ruffled her black feathers and readjusted her footing on the windowsill.

The baby looked up at the crow again, with tears rolling down her chubby pink cheeks.

The crow cawed at the child and the baby gurgled and smiled at the bird.

The crow answered and kept watch over the baby until her bleary-eyed father stumbled into the room. He saw the crow on the windowsill and shooed it away as he went over to pick up his daughter.

The tired father went through his morning chores with his daughter tucked under his arm. He made breakfast and made the bed. He got his daughter dressed for the day and all the while, the crow sat near the kitchen window and watched the baby closely.

The baby noticed the crow and her eyes stayed locked on the bird over the course of the morning.

The bond had been made.

The crow was happy and patiently waited for the father to go outside and start his morning chores.

He emerged into the morning sunlight with the baby in one arm. He carefully laid out a blanket near where he would be tending the garden and placed the baby girl down on it.

He went over to get his farm tools and started his chores, all the while keeping one eye on his baby girl.

The crow approached the blanket. The baby rolled over and started to crawl her way towards the crow, reaching out to it.

The crow approached slowly, because sometimes, if it wasn't the right baby, they could be unpredictable.

But the crow liked this child. The crow knew that she would be one of the chosen. That this child will become rich with power and magic as she grew older. The power came from her mother. It was very strong, which meant only one thing.

The crow stepped closer to the baby and lowered his head to the child.

The baby reached out and gently pet the crow's head.

The crow felt the change happen.

The tiny seed of magic had implanted itself in the child.

This was how witches were made.

The child continued to pet the crow, and the crow shuffled closer to the girl on the blanket. She giggled and gurgled with delight as the crow came even closer and looked deep into the child's eyes.

Yes, she would do nicely.

The crow let out a loud caw and called to the other crows.

Seemingly out of nowhere, the murder of crows kettled high in the sky and then came down around the girl and landed in a circle that surrounded the child.

She and her familiar stayed in the center of the circle as the other birds cawed in celebration of the choice.

The baby's father noticed the commotion and came over to see what was happening.

The crows all turned to face the father as he came running towards them swinging a long-handled shovel and yelling at them, trying to shoo them away from his child.

The murder of crows did as their name implied brought the mother's vengeance down on the man. They swarmed around the father in a mass of flapping wings, flying feathers, sharp beaks, and claws.

The child and her familiar stayed on the blanket, with the crow keeping the baby's attention from the gruesome scene mere yards away from her and her blanket.

When the fight was over, the crows came back to the blanket.

Vengeance was done.

They surrounded the child once again and then they each took part of the edge of the blanket in their beak. They flapped their wings and the blanket lifted off the ground. The baby squealed with delight as they rose into the air and the birds flew away from the tiny farm with their prize.

They flew deep into the forest until they came to a small hut that had smoke rising in purple swirls from the chimney.

The familiar landed on the kitchen windowsill and cawed a victorious note into the kitchen.

The woman came outside and saw the murder of crows coming in for a gentle landing and they laid the blanket at the woman's feet.

She was not young but was still beautiful. She tucked her long skirts out of the way as she bent over to pick up the baby.

The blanket fell open as the birds flapped away and left the woman, the baby, and the familiar to their meeting.

The other crows landed in a circle surrounding the little hut and watched.

The woman picked up the baby and stared into the child's eyes.

The baby gurgled with happiness and reached out to tug on a lock of the woman's gray hair that tumbled down over her shoulder and into the baby's grasp.

The child giggled and pulled the lock of hair hard.

"She is a strong one," the woman said to the crows. "And she has great potential, I can feel it."

She looked over at the familiar, who took off from the ground, circled around her three times and then landed on the woman's other shoulder.

The crow looked down at the baby in the woman's arms and then at the woman with an inquisitive expression.

"You chose well," the woman nodded. "And now it begins."

Yep. I do have a weird fear of marionettes. Here's why.

Marionette

The marionette was standing on the sidewalk outside of my house.

The mere sight of her filled me with disbelief and terror. I hid behind the curtains and peered out the window at her.

I always knew, somewhere in the back of my mind, that she would be back for me.

The marionette hung in the corner of my room for as long as I could remember. I don't have any idea when I got it or who I got it from. It just hung in the corner and drifted around in slow circles as she dangled from my ceiling. She was always there, watching me.

She seemed friendly, at first. She had yellow yarn hair and a face made of a round circle of wood. Her features were painted on the wood in black lines and her big blue eyes watched me. She had a smile painted on her face with rosy pink circles for cheeks.

She wore a white blouse with tiny pink, blue, and yellow flowers on it and wore blue pants that were supposed to look like bell-bottom jeans. Her wooden feet were painted black to resemble shoes and her wooden hands were the same fleshy pink color as her face.

I tried in vain a few times to play with her, but it was like she didn't want to cooperate. The cross shaped piece of wood in my hand with the strings that led down to her never quite felt right. I could never get her to do anything except a weird awkward bounce across the floor.

I tried quite a few times to make peace with her and coax her into playing with me, but she just didn't seem to want to.

So I left her hanging in the corner of my room. She hung from a hook in the ceiling that held the string from her head and was braided by the cross piece that was supposed to help to control her. It never really did control her. Not like it should have.

She scared me.

She didn't want to cooperate with me when we played and I just left her up in the corner of my room. I knew that at some point she would start to resent me. I could feel it.

I always waited for the day when she turned back around from one of her slow circles, the day when she would turn to face me and she would have a frown on her face rather than that painted on smile.

When her back turned to me, I was always terrified of what would happen next. I would sit and watch her while I held my breath and waited for her to turn around again, always expecting her expression to finally be different. It never was. She just turned to face me with that painted smile and big blue eyes.

I had horrible nightmares about her climbing down from the ceiling and killing me in my sleep. It was a recurring nightmare throughout my childhood. I never told anyone how terrified I was of that marionette. I was afraid that if I did tell someone, it would put them in danger too.

Once in a while, my mother would come into my room and say she was collecting old toys for charity and she wanted everything I didn't play with anymore.

Every single time, I tried to talk my mother into taking the marionette. And every single time, for some reason, she said no.

And then, I waited in terror for the revenge she would take for me trying to get rid of her once again. Nothing ever happened, but I was convinced that someday, it would.

I hated that marionette. I hated her so much that I never even gave her a name.

My mother called her Cindy, but I refused to call her that. It was almost like the thought of giving her a name would give her the power or acceptance that she finally needed to come to life.

This thing hung in the corner of my room until I moved out. It watched my entire childhood and knew all of my secrets. It was the only toy I had that made it from childhood to adulthood with me. All of the others were given away at some point or another.

When I finally moved out, I was unpacking my boxes at my boyfriend's house. He saw the marionette lying in a box and he looked at it and then looked at me.

"You aren't going to hang this thing up in here are you?" he asked.

I looked in the box.

She was laying there, face down, with her dusty yellow hair at the top of the box.

I shook my head and just stared at her, eyes wide with fear of an inanimate object.

"I only packed it because my mom would never let me throw it away," I said.

"Well, this thing gives me the creeps," he said. "Can I throw it away?"

"Please," I said.

I was so happy to finally have an ally against the creepy thing.

He picked it up out of the box and walked it out to the trash can outside.

I couldn't watch. I didn't want to accidentally see her face as she was taken out of the room.

I finished unpacking and sat down on the bed. I breathed a sigh of relief that for the first time I could remember, that marionette wasn't hanging in the corner of my bedroom. For the first time in my life, it wouldn't be watching me sleep.

I did have a nightmare about the marionette that night. It had made its way back into the house, it was coming towards me in my sleep. I woke up in a cold sweat, with no marionette in the room.

My boyfriend pulled the trash can out front on garbage day and I eyed the can out the window as it stood on the street with her buried somewhere deep inside.

I was so happy to have that thing out of my life for good.

I listened for the trash truck and sighed with relief as it came and went.

I looked out the window and saw that there was something lying in the street in front of our house.

It had a yellow yarn head and was wearing a white blouse and blue jean bell bottoms.

I literally shrieked in horror.

My boyfriend came to the window and looked out to see what made me scream.

He saw the tangled mass in the street and squinted out the window at it.

"What is that?" he asked.

"It's the marionette," I said.

He looked at me and then looked out at the street at the tangle of wood and string and 70's attire.

"Now that's just creepy," he said. "I'll go get it."

I grabbed him by the arm and pleaded, "Be careful."

"It's just a marionette," he shrugged. "Nothing more."

"But she doesn't want to go," I said.

"Don't be weird," he laughed. "I'll take care of it."

I watched out the window as he went out to the street and grabbed the marionette rather roughly and grabbed the trash can to pull it back to where it resided on the side of the house.

I was rather surprised when he came inside with the marionette dangling from his hand.

I checked, just to make sure that the smile was still painted on her face.

It was.

I just had to be sure.

"Here," he said. "We'll take care of this once and for all."

He walked over to the fireplace and threw the marionette into the dark opening and onto the charred pieces of wood that remained in there.

He grabbed some newspaper for kindling and stuffed it underneath the marionette.

"This will take care of things once and for all," he said as he lit a match and set the newspaper on fire.

"You're burning her?" I asked.

I couldn't believe my eyes. I would finally be rid of the thing that terrorized me for so long.

I went over to the fireplace and sat down next to him.

The newspaper went up in flames and engulfed the marionette in the orange flickering fire. The wooden cross handle went up in flames and the fire crept down the strings and towards the marionette.

I found myself holding my breath as I waited for her to disappear into the ember sprinkled ashes.

I leaned in and looked into the fireplace. What I saw made me want to get up and run. I wanted to run as far away as possible.

"Hmmm," my boyfriend leaned in towards the flames. "She must be treated with something, because she won't burn."

The marionette laid in the fireplace, completely untouched by the fire that was dying down around her.

He reached in and tried to touch her.

"Ouch," he pulled his hand away. "It's friggen hot."

"You did just set it on fire," I said.

He grabbed a fireplace poker and pulled her out onto the hearth.

The handle that controlled her and her strings had burned away, leaving the limp doll laying on the bricks in front of him.

"I gotta say, this thing is really creeping me out," he said.

That evening, some friends came over and one of them loved creepy things.

"I'll take her if you don't want her," he said. "This will make a great story to tell people when they come over and see her at my place."

"Please," I said. "She's all yours."

I almost cried with relief when he left the house with her in his hands.

It's been thirty years.

I've lived in several different states since then.

I stopped thinking about that marionette years ago.

I had intentionally forgotten her and kept her hidden away in a corner recess of my mind where I didn't dare to tread.

But now, as I stared out my window, there she is.

I don't know how she found me.

She looked like someone had tried to burn her more than once.

Her blouse was ripped at one shoulder, exposing the oddly jointed shoulder and wooden arm. Her yellow yarn hair was singed and charred black on one side as well.

Her bell bottom jeans had holes in the knees and were tattered along the bottom edges around her ankles. Her clothing was smudged and dirty, as was her face. Years of wear and tear were showing on the thing.

She stood out front, without strings to hold her up, and she glanced up and down the street.

I peered out from behind the curtains of my front windows and watched as she moved on her own, just like I knew she always could.

She looked at my house, at the window I was peering out from, and the frown I always feared would be there was painted on her face.

Gerald longed for the light of the full moon. Just so he could see her for a few brief moments. Caught in a monthly cycle of longing and grief, Gerald is tortured by the excruciating wait for the light of the full moon. A haunting and heart-string pulling short story.

In the Light of the Full Moon

Gerald sat on the old tire swing that hung from the towering oak tree at the park down the street from his house. The smell of cut grass was making his nose run and his eyes were watering uncontrollably. He wiped away the tears running down his face with his sleeve and dug a tissue out of his pocket to blow his nose.

He ran his fingers over the gritty black rubber and felt the raggedy rope that held the tire in place. He leaned back and watched the clouds drift in front of the waxing moon in the midnight sky. The naked arms of the old oak tree danced their macabre ballet in the sporadic gusts of wind that made him shiver in the cold.

It was the last night before the full moon.

He longed for these nights.

Each month the wait seemed longer and more excruciating. But that was only because the anticipation tried his patience.

He couldn't wait to see her again. The beautiful woman who only appeared by the light of the full moon.

She penetrated his thoughts every waking hour. He had gotten to the point where he couldn't concentrate. He was about to lose his job because of his obsession, but he didn't care.

Every night, as the full moon grew closer, he sat and waited for her. Even though he knew that he wouldn't see her until the moon was full. He didn't want to chance missing her.

Sometimes, just sometimes, she appeared near morning, if the full moon landed during daytime hours.

And so he waited for her on the nights before the full moon. Just in case.

As morning drew closer, he could feel his eyelids getting heavier. But Gerald fought to stay awake.

Just as the first light of the blue hour dawned, he saw her walking towards him. She was even more beautiful than he remembered. Her white dress and long dark hair were blowing in the gusts of wind that made him shiver uncontrollably through his coat. He sat frozen in place, taking in her beauty and her transparent visage.

As the sun grew higher, she disappeared in the morning mist, leaving Gerald scrambling ungracefully out of the tire swing and to where he had last seen her standing before the slightest rays of sun made her disappear once again.

He headed home, with his mind filled with thoughts of her.

Gerald got into a hot shower, and tried to chase away the chill that had penetrated all the way to his bones.

He stood there for a long time, waiting for his body to warm up and for the courage to turn off the water and face the cold and lonely winter morning.

He went through his day like a zombie. He could feel his supervisor's eyes boring into the back of his skull like a drill as he tried to focus on his work. When his supervisor finally moved along to go and stare at another hapless co-worker, he slipped away from his desk to the breakroom.

Gerald picked up the empty coffee pot and glared at it. The bright pink sticky note that read "If you finish it, refill it" stood out uselessly against the black machine.

His desire for caffeine to get through the day outweighed his ire for whoever left the pot empty and he refilled the pot. He put in triple the amount of grounds necessary and waited for the machine to run the first bit of black gold through the fresh grounds and directly into his mug.

He took his black coffee back to his desk and stared at the clock in the bottom corner of his computer.

The minutes ticked by slowly. His only morning pleasure was listening to his co-workers make noises of disgust at the extra strong coffee he had made. He smiled, in spite of himself when one co-worker in particular gagged on his cup and dumped out the remains to make a fresh pot. From years of working there, Gerald knew that was the culprit that never refilled the empty pot.

When the day had finally come to an end, Gerald was the first one out of the office. He could feel his supervisor's eyes on him once again, but he didn't care.

He had to see her and he knew the first part of the night would be the time when she would appear. The time closest to the full moon.

He raced to the park and sat in the frigid cold to wait for her to appear once again.

His hands were numb by the time she showed up. He could feel the ache up to his elbows as the piercing pain made him stuff his hands farther and farther into his pockets.

When she approached him, he knew she wouldn't see him. She never did.

He watched as her long beautiful hair floated around her like a dark halo in the silvery moonlight.

Gerald climbed out of the swing.

He had to let her have it.

So many nights before, he had tried to keep it from her. But she had to have it.

The first time he kept it from her, she turned into a girl of the age of twelve and walked out into the street that ran in front of the park and was hit by the ghost of a car, leaving her bleeding in the street.

He had tried over and over to keep her from getting on the swing. And over and over, she was killed in some horrible and new way, right in front of his eyes. All before she reached the age of thirteen.

Gerald didn't used to believe in destiny, but she made him consider the possibility.

And it made him angry.

But the anger melted away as she approached.

He moved aside so that the woman could climb onto the tire swing.

He watched as she grew younger and younger, until she was a young girl.

Seven years old, to the day, to be exact.

She leaned back as she swung higher and higher. He watched as she giggled and let her long dark hair fly out behind her as she swung. That single look of elation on her face was his one true moment of joy each month.

But then, when the swing was at its highest, the girl lost her grip, and Gerald watched in horror once again as his daughter tumbled and fell from the swing.

It took all he had to restrain himself from running to her side, like he wished he could have that day. Like he should have that day.

But he hadn't been there with her. He had stayed late at work that day. Just as he had every other day.

Gerald knew better than to go over to touch her. He knew better than to try to change the events that had already come to pass.

Any time he tried to interfere with the way things happened on that day, he never got to see his beautiful daughter the following month.

He watched with tears flowing down his face as the body of his daughter laid on the ground and slowly morphed into the beautiful woman he waited to see each month.

She stood up from her place in the grass and walked towards where he stood.

She looked at him and gave him the slightest nod and smile and then she disappeared.

Gerald knew he wouldn't see her again until the next full moon. And the agony of waiting to see her started all over again.

Contact with "alien life forms" could happen right here, on earth. Not just could, they have happened, and we know that there are undiscovered creatures out there. Just how dangerous are they?

Junior Research

I stood at the metal door that separated me from life and death. It wasn't just the monster outside that could kill me. It was the fact that if that door got breached, there would be no survival. Monster or no monster.

So, the fact that the creature was now trying to tear the door off our DSV was pretty much our biggest concern right now.

I ran towards the emergency closet and pulled out one of the big clunky suits we were supposed to wear if we were suddenly planning to exit the DSV. But considering our location, I didn't really think the suit was going to save me. Even if I was able to manage to get it on properly before the creature made its way in here to eat me.

I have always wanted to work for NASA. It was my dream. Space exploration was my primary interest. I thought it would be amazing to find alien life out there somewhere.

The biggest and best day of my teenage life was when I was able to meet with someone who worked in the space program. It was one of those things they arranged for students in high school to meet people who actually worked in their desired future occupation.

I was so excited. To me, meeting someone who worked in the space program was like meeting a rock star.

I met with this person, who has always asked to remain anonymous. Although I would think that the people who work with them would be able to figure out who they are just by the fact that they know who they have sent to which schools and when. But that part of the story doesn't matter.

What matters is that I became friends with this person. They were young and practically fresh out of school themselves. So, we became friends.

First, it was just emails going back and forth as I updated this person on my progress through school.

Then, we started to meet up occasionally. Just to talk about how things were going as I made my way through college.

Soon, we became close friends and drinking buddies.

It was one night at a bar that changed the course of my life, and my career. It was that night that brought me here, to this particular time and place.

My friend got more than a little drunk and we started talking about alien contact.

It was something we were both passionate about. And it was something that we were both very disappointed that neither one of us had come even close to encountering up to that point in time.

I had become discouraged as of late about the possibility of never encountering alien creatures in my lifetime.

The question that changed the course of my life happened almost accidentally.

The bartender was the one who asked the question. He might have asked the question as a joke, not really expecting any sort of a real answer. But it came from him just the same.

"With all the money that the space program has, why have none of the resources gone to researching our oceans? It's practically unexplored and is right here on earth."

My friend's drunken answer to the bartender wasn't exactly something that could be repeated in polite company.

After the bartender stalked off, my friend uttered the words that changed my life.

"You want to know a secret?" they asked, voice slurred from the fourth shot of tequila that we had already downed.

"Sure," I said.

"We actually have explored the oceans," they said. "Why the hell do you think we want off of this planet so badly?"

"What?" I asked, the shock of their statement totally shook my thoughts back towards sobriety. "What did they find?"

"Shhh," they put their finger to their lips and laughed. "It's top secret. I'm not supposed to tell."

It took two more shots of tequila, of which I did not partake, to get more information shaken loose from their internal top-secret file.

And that information made me change my major.

Deep-sea exploration became my one and only goal. My obsession really.

I had a burning desire to find out what was lurking in the depths of our oceans, right here on our own planet.

Contact with "alien life forms" could happen right here, on earth. Not just could, they have happened, and we know that there are undiscovered creatures out there.

It wasn't just a possibility; it was a probability.

Fine, they won't have technology or be flying around in spaceships. Their intelligence might be severely limited. But then look at how intelligent dolphins are. Not a technology-developing kind of intelligence, but the possibilities of intelligent life are there.

But it was discovering these new creatures, new life forms, that I was passionate about. So why not do it here in our own oceans?

Once I graduated, it wasn't long before I was able to get into a deep-sea exploration program. I was a junior researcher, and my job was mainly to document everything that happened on our mission. No matter how mundane.

This was my first mission, and as of 1547 this afternoon, we encountered our first unidentified deep-sea creature.

At first, we thought it was just an oversized octopus, but upon closer investigation, we realized that it wasn't an octopus. It had too many tentacles. Way too many tentacles.

And the size of the creature was astounding. It was larger than our DSV by at least three or four times.

The door of our deep-submergence vehicle creaked under the pressure of the creature that was right outside. Its long tentacles had wrapped around our DSV and the roof and walls around me were starting to dent inwards from the pressure created by the grip of the creature.

This is what I had wanted, right?

To discover new life. To go where no one had gone before?

Is this really the moment I had dreamed of since childhood?

Yeah, it really was. And I was beyond excited about it.

"Start our ascent," my boss screamed at the guy who was piloting our DSV.

I hadn't even had time to learn anyone's names yet, and here we were trying to pull some sort of massive leviathan closer to the surface so that the ship above us could try to capture it. Or stun it, or kill it.

My fear of death was in full combat with my irrational excitement of finding a new creature on my very first job as a junior researcher.

"Titan DSV 26Z has made contact and we are starting our ascent," the radio-guy said into this headset.

He was the one who kept us in contact with the ship that launched us out into the deep. It was a military ship that seemed like it was the size of a small city. It floated high above us on the surface.

It was our job to get this creature to a depth where they could send out their "retrieval pods" to capture the leviathan.

We were sent out as bait.

I listened to the metal creak and the deafening crunching sound of the walls denting around me.

It was at that moment that I realized that this DSV was not going to be powerful enough to win in a battle of what direction we went.

If the leviathan didn't want to ascend into less pressurized areas, then we weren't going there.

Our DSV was programmed to do automatic photographic, sonar, depth readings, and magnetic surveys on a constant basis. It sent all our technical and location information to the surface.

A series of red lights started flashing along the dash in front of our pilot.

"We're ascending too fast," he said.

So much for the creature not wanting to go to lower pressure levels.

As we ascended, the creature started caving in the walls of our DSV.

I watched as the first wall cracked open and I was able to get one last thought in before panic ensued and water rushed in and flooded our cabin.

"Was this really the moment I had been waiting for my entire life?"

*What happens when fantasy creatures and monsters
are addicted to humans?*

H.A.A.

Thomas entered the room cautiously. It was a
very small gymnasium that smelled of donuts and hot
coffee and feet. It was also full of creatures he had
never seen before.

There was a wood elf up at the front of the
room. She was the most beautiful creature he had ever
laid eyes on. Her long blonde hair hung down her
back in flowing waves of gold. Her pointed ears
peeked out through her hair and looked sharp enough
to be a weapon. Her ocean blue eyes locked on his as
he walked into the room.

Thomas knew all eyes were on him. He
looked human. As far as he was concerned, he still
was human. Mostly.

He could feel the eyes of the wood elf on him.
She raised her nose into the air and sniffed, almost
imperceptibly. She narrowed her eyes at him, but
nodded just slightly. Her flowing green dress trailed
behind her as she took her seat at the front of the
room.

All of the creatures took their seats among the
rows of folding metal chairs. Some sat on cushions
near the front of the room. Some were eyeing Thomas

as if they didn't trust him. But the creatures would look up at the wood elf and she would nod reassuringly at them.

The room settled into an uneasy silence as the wood elf raised her hand to quiet the room.

"My name is Aerin," she said. "For those of you who are new, I am a wood elf and I am the chair-fae in charge of running our meetings. I would like to welcome you all to this evening's meeting of Human Addicts Anonymous."

There were a few muffled claps around the room and then another awkward silence.

"I encourage all new-comers to speak at their first meeting," she eyed Thomas as she said this. "But if anyone else would like to get us started, it would be most agreeable."

She gracefully sat down on a wooden dining chair at the head of the group.

A small creature in brown overalls and a tiny bowler hat with a red glistening hummingbird feather sticking out of the band stood on his chair and cleared his throat.

"Ahem," he started. "My name is Alfrigg and I am a Human Addict."

"Hello, Alfrigg," chorused the room.

"I'm a brownie, you see," Alfrigg said. "And we tend to live with the humans. In their walls. In their homes. We see everything they do. We watch. We listen. We usually stay hidden. Completely unknown to the humans. But sometimes…"

Alfrigg stopped and took off his hat to reveal a small patch of wiry brown hair on top of his head.

"Sometimes, they discover us," Alfrigg looked ashamed. "And sometimes, they even try to make friends with us."

Alfrigg took a long pause before continuing, his voice sounded choked up as he spoke. "The last family I lived with. Their little girl discovered me. It started innocently enough. She left me milk and bread. The bread was so good. Homemade. Her mother was a baker."

Alfrigg shook his head in shame, "I started cleaning the kitchen at night. To earn my bread. You know how us brownies are, we feel bad just taking it from them, so we work. I didn't mind a little kitchen cleaning. I thought it was harmless. But then, on Sundays, the little girl would leave me a plate of honey. The good kind. Fresh from the farmer's market."

Heads nodded around the room in agreeing sympathy.

"I had to get out of there," Alfrigg said. "It was getting to be too much. I would feel compelled to vacuum and dust. I knew I had to leave when the little girl started leaving pieces of cake slathered with butter cream frosting. I found myself," Alfrigg paused to choke back tears. "I found myself cleaning their bathroom."

He sat down hard on his chair, wiping his eyes. The creature next to him patted him on the back and handed Alfrigg a hanky.

"Thank you, Alfrigg," Aerin said softly. "That was wonderful sharing. Anyone else?"

A manticore raised his hand and stood up.

"Hello, my name is Kallan, and I am a Human Addict," he said.

"Hello, Kallan," the creatures in the room said.

The manticore swished his tail out from under his feet and smoothed his hair back along his spotted head.

"I am a manticore," he started. "We are supposed to eat humans. But I fell in love with one."

Everyone in the room gasped slightly.

"She wasn't supposed to be the one," Kallan said. "She was just wandering through the forest one day. I wasn't that hungry because I had just eaten a small troop of Boy Scouts. So, I kidnapped her, to save her for later. A midnight snack, maybe."

Kallan looked around the room and swished his tail again. "But she was so kind and gentle. She was never afraid of me at all. I just couldn't eat her."

Various creatures around the room nodded sympathetically.

"So, one day, I decided to let her go," Kallan said. "But she wouldn't leave. I knew it could only end badly. So, I left. I came straight here."

Applause burst out around the room punctuated by "Good for you." and "Good call." and "We're here for you."

Kallan sat back down and Alfrigg handed him his hanky. Kallan took it and blew his nose loudly.

A siren stood up suddenly, her beautiful blue hair cascading down her shoulders and back. Thomas could see the faint outline of iridescent scales on her skin.

"Hello, my name is Rhoswen," she said in a beautiful voice. "I'm a Human Addict."

"Hello, Rhoswen."

"I have such an addiction to humans that I can't even get into my own home anymore," she said. "I sing to the ships as they pass and they crash into the cliffs. My sisters and I would feed. Everything was fine. But I couldn't stop. I crashed every ship. They've all piled up around my home and I can't get in anymore. My sisters told me I have a problem, so I came here."

Another siren went over and took Rhoswen by the hand. She whispered something to the siren and they left together into a small side room where they could speak in private.

There was another awkward silence and then Aerin spoke up.

"How about you, our newcomer," she said. "Would you like to introduce yourself?"

Thomas looked around the room. All eyes were on him.

Thomas awkwardly stood up, suddenly feeling very unsteady on his feet.

"Hi, my name is Thomas, and I'm not sure if I am a human addict or not," he said.

"Hello, Thomas," some annoyed voices said.

"I mean, I was a human," Thomas said. "I am a human, most of the time. Until recently. Apparently, the dog that bit me last month was a werewolf. And now I'm not sure where I belong. I've been trying to keep my job, but things are different, you know. I'm changing."

"You're not a human anymore," a deep voice said from the back of the room.

Thomas turned to see another man at the back of the room. Thomas hadn't noticed him when he came in. The man must have slipped in quietly just before Aerin started the meeting.

He was mid-thirties and wearing jeans and a leather jacket. He wore dark brown work boots with the laces untied and his dark hair was slicked back.

"Who are you?" Thomas asked.

"I'm Warren," he said. "And if you'd like a sponsor, you just let me know. I'm a werewolf too."

"Well, I'm still human 29 days a month," Thomas said. "Like I assume you are."

Warren shook his head, "We're not human, not anymore. And if you think you are still one, then this is definitely the right place for you. Because that means you're an addict, just like all of the rest of us."

"But I'm still human," Thomas objected. "Mostly."

Heads shook all around the room.

"I'm not?" Thomas asked.

Kallan looked up at Thomas. "You're like me. You need a clean break. If you don't, you'll never kick the habit."

Alfrigg nodded, "Cold turkey man. Or you'll end up like the siren. Homeless. Destitute. Humans will do that to you. Whether you believe it or not."

Thomas looked over at Warren. "What did you do?"

"I found a pack," Warren smiled. "You can join mine. You might have to put up with a little hazing now and again, but I think you'll fit in just fine."

Thomas looked up at the wood elf. She nodded encouragingly at him.

"You need to be with your own kind," Aerin said. "You need to learn their ways."

"The humans will just reel you in and break your heart," Alfrigg said. "You'll be scrubbing toilets before you know it."

Thomas shook his head. "I can't just leave my life."

A small dragon had been sitting in the far corner of the room. He rose to his feet and showed Thomas a stump where one of his front feet was missing. "You see this, wolf?"

The dragon made eye contact with Thomas and held his gaze, just to make sure he was listening. Thomas stared into the frightening yellow eyes that loomed two feet above him and remained silent.

"This is what happens when you trust humans for too long," the dragon said. "I made a friend. A knight. He was all right. Friendly even. We were companions for years. But then someone claimed a dragon ate their sheep. The flocks were disappearing. And then that friend. That companion. He came for me. We fought. I got the better of him, but not before he took my arm."

Thomas stared at the stump that the dragon held out to him.

"This is what staying with the humans will get you," the dragon said. "Sooner or later, someone will find out your secret, and then they will hunt you. They always do."

The dragon blew two rings of smoke out of his nostrils and then turned and went back to his corner.

Aerin looked out the window at the moon and said, "That's wonderful sharing. Thank you everyone. But our time is almost up. Sunrise is coming soon."

The creatures stood and started helping the wood elf to put the chairs away, and in hiding all evidence that they had used the room.

Thomas looked from the dragon in the corner to Warren.

"Have you been hunted?" Thomas asked. "By humans?"

Warren nodded. He looked sad about it too.

Thomas sighed and walked over to the man standing in the back of the room.

"You have a pack?" Thomas asked. "They keep you safe?"

Warren nodded.

"I'll introduce you," Warren said. "Just talk to them. Then you can decide."

Thomas nodded.

He felt a hand on his shoulder and he turned to see the wood elf, Aerin standing behind him, her ocean blue eyes staring into his.

"You're making the right decision," she said in her soft voice. "And you're welcome back to our meetings anytime."

I love playing RPG's. This was written as part of the backstory for one of my characters. A startling vision sets the stage for young Kipp, a Dragon-kin with an ominous destiny.

Hiding No More

Everything trembled and shook. Trees cracked with a horrible snap and fell, crashing to the ground. The terra firma started to crumble away as rolling waves of tremors carved away at the earth like the tides of the ocean.

Rolling black clouds clawed their way across the clear blue sky and slowly became a burning ember orange. The heavens looked as if they were on fire and ready to come crashing down to destroy everything beneath it in an incinerating rain of destruction.

The ground shook and cracked. The terrible rumbling of the ground was almost deafening. The air filled with dirt and the strong scent of freshly dug soil as the earth cracked open wide and a terrible mouth with fangs and gnashing teeth opened wide towards the ember sky.

I watched in horror as a massive dragon rose from the depths of the earth, of the land that was my home.

Although I was very young, I knew that the dragon was twisted with evil and that he served an evil even more terrible and more powerful than the massive dragon himself.

The only thing I could hear, echoing over the rumbling and the screams that filled the air, were the words "*raise the fallen.*" I didn't hear the words so much as felt them being carved into my mind with raking claws. I suddenly turned ice cold and the frozen sun continued to burn me with an icy chill that ran through my entire being.

I could look down and see villages being destroyed below. People being sacrificed on altars and being dragged towards them screaming. I could see all of the blood being spilled in honor of the dragon and in the shadow of the frozen sun.

Then I felt myself falling and being slammed back to the burning earth so hard it knocked the wind from my lungs. I heard a terrible chorus of voices rise over the sound of my village crumbling to its death, over the screams that came from the many villages that were engulfed in flames and burning to the ground. It was one word being lifted up in a unison of voices.

Malvolek.

I woke up screaming and couldn't stop until my parents were both by my side. It took them what seemed like hours to calm me down. I told them of my dream, still shaking and crying as I described the feelings of horrible icy cold that crept up my spine and burned me with its frozen flames as the dragon rose from the dying earth and as I watched hundreds, no thousands, of people dying. I described oceans of blood and sacrifice.

My parents looked at one another in horror as they realized that what I had woken up from was not just a dream, but a vision. They told me that visions were something those of us who were Dragon-kin were prone to, but no one had shown the gift in a very long time. They tried their best to lull me back to sleep, but sleep did not come easily that night for any of us.

The following afternoon, I was playing in the back room when two visitors came to the front door. My parents answered and the two visitors spoke with them. I could tell something was wrong when my parent's voices started to rise.

I peeked around a corner and saw two men in in robes standing in the doorway. I shuddered when I saw the symbol of the yellow eyed dragon on the front of their robes.

They were demanding that my parents hand something over to them and demanded that they pay tribute as well.

As my parents argued with them, I noticed another figure behind the two men in the doorway. He was silent and stood back several feet from the men at the door. He wore his hood up over his head so that I couldn't see his face.

But I could hear the thoughts of the silent hooded figure.

His mind echoed with images of my vision and were filled with thoughts of the blood sacrifice that was coming to appease and release the terrible Malvolek.

The figure immediately sensed me in his mind, and he locked eyes with me.

He forced the image of me being sacrificed to Malvolek into my mind and it caused me to scream out.

My parents heard my screams and shoved the two men out of the doorway and slammed the door in their faces.

My parents rushed to my side and calmed my screams and my tears.

My mother had an amulet that she had always worn around her neck. She took it off and placed it over my head and tucked the amulet beneath the folds of my clothes.

"Never take this off," she said to me. "Never lose it."

My father put a belt around my waist and pulled it snuggly, almost too tight. He slipped a sheathed dagger into the belt and said, "This will warn you of danger. Never part with it."

My parents kissed me and hugged me tightly as they told me where to go and hide.

They promised to come and find me when it was safe once again.

There was pounding on the front door and my parents kissed me again.

"We will always love you," they said. "And whatever you do, don't look back. Now RUN!"

I took off into the woods in the direction that my parents had told me to go. I ran for what seemed like forever. My lungs burned and tears stung my eyes as I ran.

I ran until I found the cave that my parents had told me to find, and I stayed there, hidden and waiting for my parents to come for me and take me home again.

But they never came for me.

I waited in the cave, just like I had been told, not wanting to miss my parents' return.

A few days later, a druid came and found me. I was starving and dehydrated, shivering from the cold in the cave.

She nursed me back to health, but I stubbornly refused to leave the cave.

I had to wait for my parents to return.

It wasn't until the druid told me of my parents' death and that my entire village had been sacrificed by the cult of the yellow eyed dragon, that I finally ventured forth from my cave.

As I grew, the druids took care of me and taught me things. They also kept me hidden, for fear of the yellow eyed dragon cult finding me and sacrificing me. Being a dragon-kin, I was difficult to hide among the villages filled with humans. My blue scaled skin and dragon-like face and my ever-increasing size made me stand out, even hiding under druid robes. So the druids let me remain living in my cave, hiding and waiting for the parents that would never come.

The druids taught me how to live in the woods and care for myself. They even taught me how to use my Dragon-kin abilities. They warned me never to use my real name, and for several years I was nameless.

Until one day, one of the druids finally gave me a name. I was learning how to use my dragon breath. At first, I wasn't very good at it. I would try with all my might and all that would happen was a small puff of smoke and then I would get the hiccups.

Kip, kip, kip.

That was the noise I made as I learned my breath weapon.

The druid found it amusing, and so that's what she started calling me.

So, since that day, my name has been Kipp.

I have been hidden away for years, doing nothing but hiding and trying to learn everything I could about dragon cults, Malvolek, and the shadow of the frozen sun.

The men in the robes never found me, but every once in a while, I can feel a yellow eye searching for me, guided by the hooded "thing" that I shared thoughts with on that horrible day.

I've grown tired of hiding.

So, I made a promise to my parents.

I was going to stop hiding, stop cowering from this evil cult, and I will stop them from making my vision a reality.

Even if I have to die in the process. It just won't be by their hands.

Kaylen skids off the icy road and winds up at the bottom of a hill where he finds a woman walking on the ice-covered lake. Kaylen, with a broken cell phone, has no choice but to go with her to get help. How much would you give up to save a life? Go with Kaylen in this mysterious, magical, and spine-tingling short story.

Touch

Kaylen was driving down the icy winding road towards home when his tire decided to blow out on him.

He gasped in horror as he tried to keep the car on the road, but he realized immediately that he was about to be in a wreck. His mind flashed through a million different images, and he found himself wondering if this was what people meant when they said they saw their life flash before their eyes.

He watched, with an uncharacteristic calmness, as the white snow-covered world spun around him, almost as if in slow motion. His view tilted upwards towards the dense and puffy cloud filled sky and he knew his car had skid off the road and that he was now going down the embankment. He watched the trees as they passed his windshield in the wrong direction, and a *thomp-thomping* sound filled his ears as he felt the small trees being bent over under the weight of the rapidly descending vehicle. He braced for impact and his car finally hit a tree large enough to stop his descent.

Kaylen sat for a few moments and tried to regulate his breathing. He was terrified of looking back behind him to see what kind of precarious situation he was currently in. He was still processing the fact that he was now off the road, with his windshield facing the sky. Some of the surrounding trees weren't very large, and he couldn't imagine the one that was now embedded in his trunk to be that much larger.

Kaylen dared to reach up with one hand and straighten his glasses so he could try to piece together an escape plan.

He reached over very carefully and unlocked the door. It clicked all of the locks in the car to the unlocked position. He then unbuckled his seatbelt.

With a loud *zoop*, the belt withdrew back into its resting place. Kaylen looked up into his rearview mirror and was relieved to see the trunk of a good sized tree taking up most of the space in the mirror. He could also see that the tree was bent to a horrible angle and probably wouldn't hold out for much longer.

He reached over and tried to open the door and was rather annoyed when he realized that gravity was working against him.

He pivoted in his seat and pushed against the door and carefully slid out of the car and placed his feet on the icy ground.

He slipped and fell to his knees and desperately grabbed at the pocket on the bottom of the door to keep himself from skidding down the hill himself. The door slammed on his wrist, sending a sharp pain all the way up his arm, and his fingers slipped painfully from the pocket as the door rebounded off his flesh. He slid down the slope until he made contact with yet another large tree.

Kaylen breathed for a moment, trying to quell his panic. He finally pushed himself up to his feet and found himself muddy and cold up to his waist. It was then he realized that his jacket was still in the car up the hill.

He sighed and took a moment to brush the mud from his hands onto his already ruined pants. The hill was slushy and wet, and fairly steep. And he wondered if he would be able to make it back up to the road in one piece.

He pulled his cell phone out of his muddy pants and checked it. It was soaking wet and covered with mud. The screen was cracked in a large spider webbing pattern and it wouldn't turn on.

He sighed and put it back in his pocket, more out of habit, and looked back up the steep hill. It would be an extremely cold, muddy, and slippery climb back up to the road.

He was about to head that direction when he heard a slight scream down the slope behind him.

He turned and looked down through the trees for who had made the noise.

"Hello?" he said in a loud voice. "Is someone there?"

There was no answer, so he started to walk down the hill in the general direction of the scream.

"Hello?" he called out.

Up ahead, near the bottom of the hill, there was a frozen lake. The ice was phantom white and the trees that surrounded it all leaned towards the solid water like they were contemplating crashing through the surface into the frigid water.

As he got closer, he could see someone out on the ice.

A woman wearing a dark blue cloak with the hood pulled up over her head was walking very carefully out on the frozen water. The edges of the cloak were lined with light gray fur and Kaylen thought she looked absolutely magical as she walked across the ice.

She slipped and fell and shrieked as she went down, grunting loudly as her feet flew out in front of her and her butt hit the surface.

The magic was gone.

"Hello?" Kaylen called out.

She carefully made her way to her feet and started walking on the ice once again.

Kaylen, who had grown up on the ice, knew that the current freeze wasn't going to make the surface thick enough to hold a person up for long.

"Hey," he called out to the woman. "Hey, the ice is too thin."

She continued to walk out towards the middle of the lake.

Kaylen made his way to the shoreline and tried to avoid slipping himself.

"Hey," he called out again.

The woman looked around at the frozen water beneath her and then squatted down on the ice. Kaylen watched as she placed her hand on the cold cloudy surface and then the ice started to crack out from her hand, spider webbing out like the crack on the screen of his phone.

"Hey," he called out again, starting to panic. "You're going to fall in."

No sooner than the words left his mouth, the woman tumbled forward through a hole that had melted through the ice.

Kaylen jumped down the steep embankment and ran across the ice, slipping and sliding the whole way, trying not to think about the fact that he could easily fall through himself at any moment.

He ran over to the hole and looked for any sign of the woman.

He could see her hood as she rose to the surface. He grabbed her and pulled her up onto the ice, breathing heavily as he dragged her to safety.

"What are you doing?" she pulled away from him. "Let go."

He stared at her in amazement when he saw that she was bone dry.

She stood up and looked down at him as he laid there on the ice, breathing heavily.

"How are you-" he gasped. "Why aren't you wet?"

"Why are you all muddy?" she asked him, staring down at him with a confused look on her face.

"My car went over the edge," he pointed feebly towards the direction he came from. "I slid down the hill."

"You were just in an accident," she said matter-of-factly.

Just then, there was a loud crack.

Kaylen and the woman both looked towards the direction that Kaylen had pointed and then Kaylen's car came rushing backwards down the hill. The car, and the tree that it had hit to stop its downward descent, both crashed through the icy water at the edge of the lake.

The car wobbled back and forth as it straddled the tree, and then popped off of it in the deep water at the edge. The car slid off the tree and sunk into the water sideways and disappeared into the inky black.

"No," she lurched forward towards the car.

"Stop," he grabbed her by the pant leg and she almost crashed down to the ice. "It's just a car. And I was alone."

"Stop touching me," she pulled her leg from his grip.

"Sorry," he said, holding his hands up in the air.

"You don't understand," she said helplessly.

Kaylen and the woman watched until the car disappeared and then looked back at one another.

Her eyes were wide as she stared down at him.

"Flat tire," he said feebly.

"It's deep there," she said. "I can't help."

She looked at him sadly.

"I know," Kaylen said. "My friends and I used to tie a rope to that old oak," Kaylen pointed to a large tree that was gnarled and bent out over the steep edge. "We'd swing out over the water and swim there. Best swimming spot on the lake."

She stared over where the car was still sending bubbles up to the surface.

"Not anymore," she said. "No one will want to swim there anymore."

"It's deep," he said. "Even if we can't get the car out, people could still swim over there."

She looked back at the hole in the ice. She went towards it and he tried to scramble to his feet to block her from the hole.

He crashed down onto the ice and stared up at her.

"What are you doing?" she demanded.

"I'm not going to let you get into that water again," he said.

She looked over at where the car had disappeared under the water and back down at him sadly. "Get up."

He reached his hand out to her and she just stared at him.

He sighed and grunted as he stood up unsteadily on the ice.

"I live near here," she said. "Let's get you inside where it's warm."

Kaylen nodded and numbly followed her as they made their way across the ice. It was slippery going, so neither one of them spoke as they carefully picked their way across.

When they reached the shore, she pointed off to the right of where they were standing.

"This way," she started through the woods.

"Hey," Kaylen said as he followed her. "How are you not wet?"

She walked quickly ahead of him, but didn't respond.

"Hey," he reached out and tapped her shoulder.

She stopped and slapped his hand away from her as she turned to face him.

"Don't touch me," she snarled.

"Sorry," Kaylen said, pulling his hand back and crossing his arms in front of himself for warmth. "I didn't mean-"

"I can't hear you when you're behind me," she said. "We need to get you warm. Now."

She started walking down the path once again.

Kaylen was shivering and his teeth were chattering as he followed her. His hands and feet were painfully cold and he just prayed that he didn't freeze to death before they got where ever it was they were going.

He tried to focus on anything but the cold. He watched as her cloak billowed out behind her as she walked. He noticed that there didn't seem to be any mud or sign of being wet from the snow on it at all as it brushed along the ground behind her.

Kaylen followed her quietly until they came to a small log cabin that had light shining through all of the windows and dark smoke rising from the chimney.

All he could think about was getting warm.

She opened the door and led him inside.

The warmth of the cabin enveloped him like a hug and he quickly went over to stand in front of the fireplace.

"Take off the muddy clothes," she commanded. "I'll get you something dry to wear."

She disappeared into a small room off to the right.

Kaylen looked around for a bathroom and saw none. He didn't want to leave the warmth of the fireplace anyway. He shrugged and decided that he'd better get his wet clothes off.

He unbuttoned his shirt and was peeling it off as the woman reentered the room and handed him some clothes.

"These should do," she said.

Her cloak was gone and her long dark hair flowed down over her shoulders in waves. She was wearing black jeans and a thick black and gray sweater.

"I don't care what they are," Kaylen said gratefully. "As long as they're dry."

He peeled off the rest of his wet clothes and pulled on the jeans and sweatshirt that the woman had given him. The sweatshirt was dark gray and fit him perfectly. He pulled on some warm socks over his bare feet and felt warmer and better already.

Kaylen stood in front of the fireplace and was happy to be dry again.

The woman came over and retrieved his muddy clothes.

"You're lucky I never throw anything away," she said as she looked him over.

She carried his clothes to a closet next to the kitchenette she had in one corner of the room. She opened the door and there was a small stacked washer and dryer where she threw his clothes unceremoniously into the open topped washer and turned it on.

Kaylen held up his cracked cell phone that he had retrieved from his pocket before he had changed clothes and held it up.

"Do you have a phone I could borrow?" he asked.

She walked over to a shelf by the front door and grabbed a cell phone and tossed it to him.

He looked at it helplessly and then back up at her.

"I don't know my friend's number," he said in dismay.

"Let's finish getting you warm and then we can look up whatever you need on my computer," she said. "Sit in front of the fire and thaw out."

She went over to the stove and put on a kettle of water.

"Hey, what's your name?" he asked.

She came over and stood in front of him.

"I'm hard of hearing," she said. "So if you want me to understand what you're saying, we have to be looking at each other."

"Oh, sorry," Kaylen said. "I didn't know."

"Of course you didn't," she said "How could you?"

"My name is Kaylen," he held out his hand to her. "What's yours?"

She stared at his hand, but didn't take it. She looked at the palm-side of his hand curiously and then looked up at him, "Wren."

"Wren," he repeated. It was a habit of his, so he would remember people's names when he met them. "It's nice to meet you, Wren. And thank you for helping me. I would have frozen to death out there."

"Do you want something to eat?" she asked.

"Uh, sure," he said. "I guess I'm going to be here a little while, huh?" He pointed at the washing machine.

She half-smiled and went over to the stove again.

There was a large cast iron pot on the stove and she ladled something out of it and into a wooden bowl. She grabbed a spoon and carried it over to him.

"This should warm you up," she said.

Kaylen was grateful to have a steaming hot bowl of what looked like some sort of meat and vegetable stew with a thick dark gravy.

"Wow," he said, taking the spoon from her that she held out to him. "This smells great, thank you."

"I made it myself," Wren said. "I hope you like it."

Kaylen took a large spoonful and lifted it to his mouth.

He regretted it instantly.

"Hot," he said, breathing through his mouth quickly to cool the contents.

"It just came off the stove," Wren said.

Kaylen felt stupid as she turned back to the tea kettle.

She brought him over a steaming cup of tea and set it on a little table that stood next to his chair.

"That one is hot too," she grinned and went back over to the stove.

Kaylen took another spoonful of stew and blew on it before inserting it into his mouth. This time, it was a decent temperature and he could taste the stew instead of just searing his mouth.

"That's really good," he said through a full mouth.

"I take it that means you like it?" she asked, laughing at him.

"Sorry," he hadn't thought that she couldn't hear him with his mouth full. He chewed and swallowed and tried again. "That's really good."

"Thank you," she smiled and sat down in a cozy looking chair across from him in front of the fire.

She started to eat a bowl of stew herself, and she stared at him intently.

"So, you read lips?" Kaylen asked.

"Today I do," Wren nodded. "I can hear sounds, but they don't always make sense in my brain. If I read a person's lips while they speak, it helps my brain connect the sounds to recognizable words."

"Oh," he said. He hesitated before saying, "So you're not-" He paused, not wanting to offend her.

"Deaf?" she finished for him. "It's not a bad word, you know. And no, I'm hard of hearing, not deaf."

"Oh," he said again. He squirmed a little bit in his chair, feeling like he had stepped into dangerous and unfamiliar territory. He had more questions, but he didn't want to offend. So he changed the course of the conversation.

"What were you doing out there on the ice?" he asked her. "And why weren't you wet when you came out of the water?"

"Magic," she shrugged.

"No," Kaylen laughed. "Really. What were you doing?"

"I just told you," Wren said as she took a bite of her stew. "Magic."

"There's no such thing as magic," Kaylen said.

"Suit yourself," Wren shrugged. "But you saw for yourself that I was dry."

Kaylen stared at her for a moment, and then took another bite of his stew while he thought about what she had just said.

"What kind of magic?" he asked.

"Which one?" she asked.

"What do you mean which one?" he asked, feeling confused, like maybe she heard the question wrong.

"What kind of magic was I doing out on the ice?" she asked. "Or what kind of magic kept me dry?"

"There are different kinds of magic?" Kaylen asked.

He wasn't sure if he should believe her or not.

"Of course there are," she laughed. "That's like asking if there's more than one field of science."

"But science is real," Kaylen said.

"And so is magic," Wren shot back. "You saw it yourself."

"I don't know what I saw," Kaylen shrugged. "But it wasn't magic. There has to be some sort of scientific explanation."

"Who says magic isn't just undiscovered science?" Wren asked. "Or at least undiscovered by scientists."

He just stared at her, unable to answer her question in his own mind.

"My cloak keeps me dry," she said. "It was given to me by my grandmother. It's been handed down through my family for generations. I don't know who initially cast the spell on it, but it's powerful magic."

"I don't believe in magic," Kaylen said stubbornly. "There must be more to it than that."

"I'm sure there is," Wren said. "But my magic isn't that strong yet. I'm still learning."

"Is that what you're doing out here, all alone in a cabin in the woods?" he asked, waving his spoon in the air, gesturing to the room around them.

"Yes, actually, it is," she stared up at him. "But I'm learning without a teacher, so it is slower going than I would like."

"Where's your teacher?" he asked.

"My grandmother died when I was young," she said. "And my mother passed away fairly recently."

"I'm sorry," Kaylen felt bad for her. "I lost my dad a few years back. Sometimes it's rough."

She just nodded.

"I have my mother and my grandmother's books," she said. "It's almost like having them here. But-"

She stopped.

Kaylen sat and ate his stew as they both watched the fire for a few minutes in silence.

He finished his tea and set the cup back on the table.

She picked it up and stared into the cup with a frown.

"The ice was way too thin to hold your weight. You know that, right?" he finally said.

"I was trying to stop someone from dying," she said. "But I was too late. Although I'm not sure why."

"Who were you trying to save?" he asked.

She just looked up at him and gave him a grim look.

"Are you reading my tea leaves?" he asked.

She nodded.

"What are they telling you?" he asked.

"That my foretelling skills need some work," she said quietly.

"My tea leaves are telling you about you?" he asked. "That doesn't seem right."

She shrugged. "It's not an exact science."

"Reading tea leaves isn't exactly science," he laughed.

"That you know of," she said. "Unfortunately some fortelling is less exact than others."

"Like whatever brought you out to the ice?" he asked.

"I didn't get the vision until it was too late," she said. "I might have been able to change things, but then I was interrupted."

"I'm sorry," Kaylen said. He didn't believe in all the hocus-pocus she was talking about, but he felt bad that he interrupted her from doing something she felt was important. "Was the person someone close to you?"

She looked up at him, "Yes, very close."

"Can we go back and finish whatever it was you were doing?" he asked.

"I can't finish it the same way," she said. "I will have to do a different sort of magic to fix it."

"So let's do that," he said.

"I'm afraid it will still be too late," she looked at him sadly. "But I do need to repair the damage I've done."

"You're not going to have to go into the water again, are you?" he asked.

"No," she shook her head. "Like I said, I just have to repair the damage I've done by not completing my first spell properly."

Kaylen was curious about what she was going to have to do. And no matter how weird he thought her beliefs were, he had a strange urge to help her. He had a strange feeling that he *knew* her.

She stood up and went across the room to rummage around in a closet near the door.

"Here," she said. "Put these on."

She handed him a pair of boots and a heavy jacket.

He slid them on and they fit perfectly.

She left the room and came back wearing her dark blue cloak.

"Who did these belong to?" he asked as he zipped up the coat.

"They're mine," she said absently. "I accidentally bought them too big."

"Why didn't you return them?' he asked.

She just shrugged.

"Let's get going," she said. "We don't have much time."

"Can you still save the person that you wanted to save?" he asked.

"We need to hurry," she said.

She opened the door and they went out into the cold.

This time, Kaylen didn't seem to be as cold as he was on his way to Wren's house. He determined that the fact that he was dry helped the situation a lot.

After a few minutes, they returned to the edge of the lake.

Wren started out onto the ice.

"Wait, stop," he said.

"We can't see from here," she said, looking back at him. "It will be fine. You have to follow me."

"You're nuts," he said, carefully stepping out onto the ice.

They made their way past where trees arched out to block their view of where his car had crashed through the surface of the lake.

There were red blinking lights coming from up the hill and a swarm of people were looking over the edge of the lake at the hole that his car had made through the ice.

"Hey," he called out. "I'm over here."

There were rescue workers coming out of the water.

Other members of their team hoisted them up the steep embankment and pulled them to safety.

The rescue team pulled something out of the water. Kaylen tried to see what it was, but there were too many men on the shore.

The men who came out of the water were just shaking their heads.

He watched in horror as he realized they had retrieved a body from under the frigid water.

He turned back to look at Wren.

"Is that?" he could feel the tears welling up in his eyes. He choked them back. "Is that me?"

"I was too late," she said. "I'm sorry. But to continue on, you had to see."

"How? What? How?" Kaylen didn't know what question to ask first.

"I got a vision," she said. "Of a car going over the cliff."

"Me," he said.

She nodded.

"What were you going to do from all the way over here?" he asked.

She shook her head.

"You were already unconscious," she said. "Up there. In the car."

"But what were you going to do from here?" he asked.

"My power can travel through water," she said. "I could have used the water to rescue you."

"How did I interrupt you then?" he asked. "We watched the car fall into the ice together. Was I already dead?"

"No," she shook her head, "I could have used the water to save you. But only if I had been able to start the spell before you hit the water."

"But I interrupted you," Kaylen said.

She nodded.

"How?" Kaylen asked.

"You must have had an out-of-body experience?" She shrugged. "That's my best guess."

"Why couldn't you still save me?" he asked.

She stared at him with tears in her eyes.

"You touched me," she said sadly.

"I had to pull you from the water," Kaylen said.

"I will have to try again next time," she said.

"What do you mean?" Kaylen asked.

"I've had visions of you before," she said.

"Me?" Kaylen asked. "Why me?"

"Because, we were meant to be together," she said, staring at her gloved hands.

"What?" Kaylen was confused. "How were we meant to be together if I'm dead?"

She looked up at him with tears in her eyes.

"It's my family's curse," she said. "I know who I am meant to be with, but he will forever get taken away."

"You know me?" Kaylen said in disbelief. "How?"

"I've saved you before," she said.

"What?" Kalyan said. "How? I've never been this close to death before."

"That you remember," she said.

"I think that would be a hard thing to forget," he said.

She stared down at the ice.

"He's coming," she whispered.

"Who?" Kaylen asked.

A man suddenly appeared next to them. He was strangely tall and very lanky. He was dressed in all black and had a dark hood up over his head. The space under the hood was pitch black, and Kaylen couldn't see the man's face or any features beneath the hood. The man stared down at them both.

"Do you want to try again, Wren?" the man asked. "Or shall I just take him now and we can end all of this?"

She looked up at the man with tears streaming down her cheeks.

"I will never stop trying until I break the curse," she said.

"You know what that means, don't you?" the man said.

Wren nodded sadly.

"Is it still worth it?" the man asked.

"Is what still worth it?" Kaylen asked. "Who are you?"

The hood turned to look at Kaylen.

Kaylen stared into the blackness and felt an emptiness as it began to fill him.

"I'm Death," he said. "And you touched her."

"What?" Kaylen asked.

"It's part of the curse," Death said.

"What is part of the curse?" Kaylen asked.

"She will forfeit half of her sense of touch to try again," Death said. "And she will never again feel your touch, no matter the circumstances. Unless she can break the curse."

Kaylen looked at Wren.

"Is that why you can't hear me?" Kaylen asked. "Is that why you're hard of hearing?"

Wren nodded. "You sang to me one time."

"Just stop," Kaylen said. "I'm not worth it."

"I love you," Wren said. "I know you don't remember, but I do."

Kaylen looked at the clothes he was wearing.

"Are these mine?" he asked.

Wren nodded.

"I'll find you again. I won't be late next time," Wren said. "I promise."

"Wait," Kaylen reached out to Wren and touched her face with his hand.

She shut her eyes, to feel his touch for the last time, as he stroked her cheek with his fingertips.

When Wren opened her eyes, Kaylen and Death were gone.

I don't delve into scifi very often, but when I do, I have a lot of fun with it.

Micah Adler was on vacation. 48 hours alone in the woods in a cabin his father used to take him to as a child. But the first night, something happened out in the woods. A crashed object out in the snow-covered woods causes a major disruption to Micah's vacation. And his life. A spine-tingling scifi short story that will leave you with chills.

Number 37

My name is Micah Adler. I am officially on vacation as of 5:01 PM yesterday afternoon.

I haven't been on vacation in over seven years. My boss always found some phony reason or other that made it crucial to the company that I not take any time off.

So, finally sick of it all, I put in a last-minute request for the weekend off while my boss was away on vacation himself. The HR department didn't see any reason to say no since I wasn't technically supposed to work weekends anyway. So here I am.

Finally.

And the HR department knows that I am "officially unreachable." No cell reception. No Wi-Fi. No TV or cable or DSL. No electronic devices of any kind.

Just me and my ever-growing TBR pile of paperback books and the beauty of nature nestled in for winter.

It will be a welcome relief.

Last night I drove straight from the office to a small cabin in the woods that my father used to take me to when I was a boy. I already had my suitcase packed and in the trunk of the car, ready to go as soon as it hit 5:00 PM.

I'm not sure what time I finally got here, but when I did, I fell face first on the bed and fell asleep immediately.

I was awoken from a deep sleep by a loud bang. It startled me into a standing position in the darkness. I would've brushed it off as just a nightmare, but the whole cabin was still reverberating from the impact. I could hear the pots and pans in the kitchenette rattling against one another in metallic annoyance.

I went to the window to look outside, but all I could see was the pitch black of night. It had started snowing and I could see the flakes as they fell towards the window in the wind.

I dropped the curtain back into place and checked my watch.

It was just after 5:30 AM.

The sun wasn't up yet, but I was. In fact, 5:30 was sleeping in for me.

I started with making some coffee.

I checked the coffee maker for cleanliness. It was probably the same old piece of junk my father used when he brought me here as a boy, but it was still cleaner than the one at work.

I filled it and set it to brewing and then I turned to tackle stoking up the fire in the fireplace.

The cabin was getting colder as the snow fell and I wanted to get it warm and toasty in here before I started my day. The owner had left the fire going for me, so it was warm when I got here. But I had ignored tending to it when I arrived, and it had waned in strength through the night.

After fumbling around for a while, I finally got the fire back going. It wasn't as easy as my dad used to make it look.

I felt a surge of victory when it finally blazed up and I set the metal screen in front of the opening as the fire cracked and popped to life. I could feel the warmth already, and it was truly feeling like I might actually be on vacation.

I poured myself a cup of coffee and went over to the little mini fridge in the corner.

The cabin was a small single room that looked like it hadn't had any work or redecorating done since the 1970's.

I didn't care because I was not here for the ambiance. I was here for the quiet.

I was especially appreciative that the owner had stocked the fridge for me like I asked him to. It was definitely worth the extra money to be standing in front of a stocked fridge and pantry at 5:30 in the morning.

I grabbed some eggs and bacon and then stared at the one burner hot plate that I had to work with. I knew my dad used to cook for two on this ancient thing. If he could cook for two, I could certainly cook for one.

I grabbed a pan and started some bacon cooking on one side of it.

While I was waiting for the single burner to heat up, I poked around in the cabinet for other necessities. I found a plate, a cup for some OJ, and even a toaster.

I looked around for an outlet and found one on the wall behind the tiny little kitchenette table. I set the toaster on the table and climbed underneath to plug it in.

When I stood up, I looked out the window and saw the first hint of sunrise.

The blue hour, I think it's called.

Memories of spending time in this little cabin with my father came rushing back to me.

I recalled some of the outdoorsy skills and information about nature that he used to tell me while we were here. I couldn't remember much of it, but I felt I could remember enough to get me through the weekend.

I do remember that I loved it here and never wanted to leave. Because of our trips here, I wanted to be a forest ranger when I was a kid. But somehow, I got stuck in the city with a job I hate and a boss that I hated even more.

The sky was clearing, and the snow had stopped. I stared out at the beautiful white landscape and reminded myself to park my car around back so I wouldn't obstruct my view out the largest window while I was here.

I took a sip of my coffee and listened to the bacon as it started to sizzle behind me on my little stove.

I noticed some movement in the faint light, and it drew my attention from the trip down memory lane and the smell of bacon as it just started to overtake the smell of the coffee.

A deer poked its head over a bush and looked over at the cabin. I still had the lights low, so I could see out the window, but I wasn't sure whether or not it could see me. I stayed very still and just watched as it meandered around, probably looking for food after last night's storm.

It stayed in view for quite a long time, and I had to break away to flip my bacon and concentrate on what I wanted to do with my eggs.

When I returned to the kitchen table to put some bread in the toaster, I noticed that the deer was laying on the ground a few yards from the back of my car.

I set my coffee mug on the table and ran outside.

I was still in my work clothes from the day before, sans tie and blazer. My shoes were not meant for snow-covered ground traction, and I promptly slipped and fell very ungracefully onto my back on the gravel driveway. The snow wasn't thick enough to do anything to cushion my fall, and I laid there with the icy snow soaking through my clothes while I berated myself for not thinking about my clothing choice for being in a rustic cabin.

As I hoisted myself back to my feet, I looked over at the deer, who decided my presence was enough reason to stand up herself. She got to her feet much more gracefully than I did, even considering the fact that she slipped in the snow herself several times.

We both got to our feet at around the same time and the deer looked at me.

Her pupils were burning with an eerie green light.

I tried to take a closer look, but she turned and bounded back into the forest.

I made my way back into the cabin and flipped my bacon once again before it burned. I was always an over-flipper when it came to cooking bacon.

I peeled off my wet clothing and put on more appropriate cabin clothes. Jeans, a white t-shirt, a red and black checked flannel shirt, and thick wool socks with a brand-new pair of hiking boots.

Much better.

I finished making my breakfast and sat at the table staring out the window contemplating the possibilities that would cause a deer's eyes to look like they were glowing green.

As I watched the sun rise through the window, I decided it was a trick of the light and dismissed the whole thing while I ate my breakfast.

Later that morning, I was laying on the couch and reading one of the many books I brought with me. I had a bowl of cheese-flavored popcorn and yet another mug of coffee within arm's reach while I stretched out in front of the fire.

My mind kept wandering back to the deer.

I decided to get up and go for a walk to clear my head.

I also wanted to see how much had changed in the area since the last time I had visited.

I donned weather appropriate clothing and headed out into the slush that was now beginning to replace the snow in the gravel driveway in front of the cabin.

The morning sun was quickly melting the layer of white that had covered the ground so beautifully earlier that morning.

I took a deep breath and smiled as I exhaled all of the stress that had been building up over the last few months.

All I wanted to focus on was the small pile of paperback books I had stuffed in the bottom of my suitcase and the beauty of nature that lay stretched out before me. I tried to erase the thoughts of work that lingered in the recesses of my mind.

The sunrise had already come and gone, and the sun was creeping higher up in the sky.

The snow that was down the path was still a blinding white.

I looked at my car, which was still completely covered with several inches of melting snow and wondered if the crash in the night had something to do with the storm.

I decided to head down the path and take a walk for a few minutes and enjoy the sights and smells of nature.

My breath drifted up from my mouth in white clouds as I breathed, and I could feel my throat drying out from the cold dry air.

I walked all the way to the end of the long and winding driveway that led to my little cabin, taking in the sites of the snow-covered trees, and listening to the morning silence.

It wasn't until I got to the road that I realized that there were no sounds coming from the woods that surrounded me. I relished the silence at first, but then I started to think that it was unnervingly quiet. I initially chalked it up to the fact that there could be another storm coming and turned to head back to the warmth of the cabin.

As I walked down the road, I saw a deer in the woods, just a few yards off the path. I stopped and stared at the magnificent creature as it slowly looked around. It was a different deer from this morning. This one was male and had a magnificent set of antlers that hadn't fallen yet this winter. It turned its head and saw me. He locked eyes with me, and I saw that same thing that I had seen in the doe's eyes earlier that morning.

The deer's eyes were glowing an eerie green. I had to do a double take to make sure that I was really seeing green glowing eyes on a deer.

As it continued to stare at me, I decided that it wasn't a trick of the early morning light. It gave me cold shivers up and down my spine that had nothing to do with the morning temperature. I picked up my pace and hurried back towards the cabin.

By the time I got there, I had convinced myself that I hadn't really seen a deer with eerily green glowing eyes at all. I just repeated to myself that it was a case of being overworked combined with a trick of the light against the melting snow.

I went back inside and took off the layers of clothes I had added on to go outside. As I took off my boots, I was reminded of when I was a boy and had to take off so many layers before I could sit down at my desk at school. That's how I suddenly felt as I hung my scarf on the hook by the door.

I could once again feel the years melting away and the stress dissipating already.

It was just a trick of the light. That's all.

I got myself another cup of steaming black coffee and went over to the window as I took the first few sips out of my mug.

Off in the distance, I could see the deer poking its head around the side of my car. It stared in the window at me, as if the green eyes were scanning me. I felt like they were penetrating me, looking straight into my soul, and I was afraid it was finding nothing left there anymore.

My thoughts of school and being a boy again crashed down around me as I stared back at the deer. It continued to stand there, staring in my direction, until I couldn't take it anymore and walked away from the window.

I sat back down on the couch and picked up my book once again.

It was just a trick of the light. It was just stress.

Deer don't have green eyes that glowed against the backdrop of the melting snow.

They just don't.

I couldn't focus. My thoughts kept drifting back to the deer.

I stood up and looked back out the window.

I gasped as I saw that the deer had ventured up towards the cabin and was standing only a few yards away from the window I was looking out of and it stared in at me with those glowing green eyes.

They were real. There was no doubt about it. The deer's eyes were glowing green, and they seemed to be getting brighter.

Before I could do anything else, the deer collapsed on the gravel driveway.

As it lay on the ground, I could see something on its back.

I set down my coffee and went to the door.

I took a deep breath and opened it, terrified of what I would find outside.

The deer was still on the ground, its chest heaving as it seemed to be gasping for air.

It moved its head so it could see me as I approached.

There was a thick dark line down the deer's back that seemed to be moving. It looked like a solid mass, stretching down the deer's back, but it undulated and moved like the waves of the ocean.

As I got closer, I could see that whatever it was on the deer's back was eating its way into the animal's spinal column. I could see that the flesh was torn, and the black line filled the gap that was down the center of the animal's back.

The deer suddenly lurched on the ground and staggered to its feet. It looked at me again and then ran back off into the woods.

I chased it for a moment, for whatever reason, but stopped running when I reached the tree line at the side of the driveway.

The deer was gone.

I didn't know what I would have done had I caught it, but it just didn't seem right to leave a wounded animal out there on its own.

I started to follow the footprints in the snow that still lay white under the trees and hoped I could be of some assistance to the poor creature.

But after a few minutes of following the trail, I found myself too cold to go on any longer and turned back to the warmth of the cabin.

Whatever was wrong with the deer was nature's way of thinning out the herd. I had no abilities or knowledge of how to save him anyway.

I thought about calling the owner of the cabin, but then remembered that I had no cell service. I would have to drive all the way into town to let anyone know about the deer.

When I got back to the cabin, I sipped my coffee and took in the layout of my single room abode.

It was everything I thought needed to get away from the city.

A warm fire, a hot cup of coffee, enough room to eat, sleep, and read for two whole days, and best of all, no phone service or internet.

That meant that my boss couldn't contact me.

Which was a dream come true.

But it also meant I couldn't contact anyone else.

I couldn't call for help. I couldn't call anyone about the deer. And I certainly couldn't call anyone if I needed help for myself.

For the first time that morning, I was wishing I had a way to contact the world without a 45-minute drive through slush and snow.

I stared at the single burner hotplate I had to work with in the circa 1970's orange and green kitchenette and started another pot of coffee.

I tried to read some more, but I was once again too distracted by thoughts of the deer.

For what seemed like the 500th time that morning, I looked at my cell phone. I was once again reminded that there was no service, and that I was here because I wanted to detox from technology and the rest of the world for 48 hours.

I set the phone aside and tried to enjoy my book in the quiet. With nothing to scroll through and nothing to watch, I was keenly aware that I was truly alone for the first time in years.

I thought back to my childhood when I dreamed of moments like this. As an introvert at heart, I relished the moments when every member of my family was out of the house, and I had the place to himself.

I loved the quiet.

I loved to read.

And I loved not having to answer to anybody while I did so.

But now things were feeling creepy.

First with the crash outside in the middle of the night.

Now with the two deer with the glowing green eyes. Both of which collapsed.

I wondered if the doe had the same gash on her back with the black line that undulated under her skin.

I started to think about the crash again. Something had hit the ground. Something big. Something big enough to rattle the pans in the cabinets.

I got up and put on my outdoor gear once again and headed outside.

The sun was much higher and was melting off the last of the snow.

It was still cold enough to see my breath as it floated away from my face in whisps.

I had no idea which direction to go to find where the noise originated from.

I tried to remember what my father had taught me about tracking things. I looked around and saw birds hopping from branch to branch in the trees while they chattered noisily. Except it was silent in one particular direction. It was as if the birds were avoiding it.

So that was the direction I headed. If it was somewhere the birds were avoiding, it must be the place. Although, if I was a smarter man, I might have followed their example.

But I trudged through the forest, with the slushy and melting snow dropping off branches as I went. Icy cold water dripped down on me as I walked, but I continued on into the eerie silence.

The forest was completely quiet in the area I was walking through. There wasn't an animal anywhere to be seen.

I was about ready to give up and head back to the cabin as my fingers and feet were starting to hurt from the cold, even through my winter clothing. But then I heard something.

It was a clicking or a chittering sound of some sort. I followed the sound until I found an area where everything was dead. The trees had fallen outward in a circle, and all looked like they had been toasted dry. The whole area was brown and perfectly dry, despite the melting snow all around it.

The entire area was completely devoid of life of any sort. And the area of death was a complete circle around a crater in the middle.

Right in the middle of the crater was a metal object of some kind.

At this point, I should have turned back around the way I came, gotten into my car, and gone to the authorities.

But no, I was too much of the curious type.

I cautiously picked my way through the fallen trees and went over to the edge of the crater.

The metal object was unidentifiable as to what it might be, but it was relatively small. About the size of a beach ball. The bottom portion, where it had hit the ground, was smashed to bits with one side torn open from the impact. The top portion had small protrusions, almost like the fins and tail of a fish.

I heard the chittering noise again, but it wasn't coming from the crash-landed fish ball.

I looked around and saw a rabbit, with green glowing eyes, staring at me over the top of a fallen pine tree.

I made my way over to the rabbit, as it fell to the ground and thrashed its legs in the loose pine needles and dirt beneath it.

When I got close enough, I could see the dark line down the rabbit's spine. It undulated and moved just like on the back of the fallen deer.

I cautiously stepped towards it, even though every fiber of my being was telling me to run.

The chittering noise was coming from inside the rabbit.

I tried to turn. I wanted to run.

But the chittering was almost like it was hypnotic. Calling me to come closer to the fallen rabbit that thrashed around on the ground.

I watched as the rabbit finally stopped moving and the undulating started to exit the creature's body.

A line of black chittered and flowed towards me.

I stood frozen in place and watched in horror as whatever it was started to come closer.

It was like watching a huge clump of tiny spiders moving towards me in a tight wave. Their movement created an ocean-like effect as they made their way over fallen trees and the dry ground in a fluid motion.

The terror I was feeling finally exceeded the hypnotic effect of the chittering and I burst into flight mode.

I ran through the forest as fast as I could to get back to the cabin.

Unfortunately, I was out of shape and halfway back, I was so out of breath that I had to slow to a jog for fear of my heart beating out of my chest and sending me into a long overdue heart attack.

As I leapt over a naturally fallen tree, I tripped over something large on the other side.

I fell sprawling into the dry pine needles and dirt in front of me.

I tried to catch my breath, but the panic of the dry ground sent another shot of adrenaline through my body.

I turned and looked at what I had fallen over. The doe I had seen earlier was laying on her side, not breathing. I took a closer look as I got to my feet and shockwaves flooded my system as I saw that the deer was totally dehydrated, almost mummified, where she lay.

I couldn't be positive that it was the same deer, and I didn't want to wait around to find out. I pushed on and made my way back to the cabin.

Once I made it back, I ran inside and bolted the door behind me. I searched madly for my car keys and in a blind panic, still breathing heavily, I tore the place apart looking for them.

I couldn't breathe. I couldn't think. I had to calm down.

I looked out the window at my car and remembered that I had left them in the vehicle. My hands had been full when I came inside, and I only brought the key to the cabin inside with me.

I went for the door but stopped when I looked out the window.

Animals were encircling the cabin, with my car on the far side of the circle.

There were more deer, rabbits, even a fox, and, most startlingly, a cougar.

They all sat surrounding the cabin and stared in the window at me. Each one had glowing green eyes.

They sat in a circular barrier between me and my car.

Out of habit, I grabbed my cell phone and looked at it once again. And once again I remembered that there was no signal in these mountains.

I chucked my phone across the room, and it landed on the bed.

There had to be some sort of emergency phone. I searched madly through the closet and in every place where a gadget could be found. I was hoping for a shortwave radio or a sat phone. Anything I could possibly use to call for help.

There was nothing.

I tried to regulate my breathing in my panic. It was all I could do to hold it together.

I looked out the window and the sky was getting overcast. There was supposed to be another storm tonight.

It didn't take long for the snow to start out of nowhere.

I looked out the window and the animals started to draw back into the woods.

I breathed a sigh of relief as I watched them back away.

I waited for them to get far enough back, planning to make a break for the car when they did.

It was getting colder by the minute, so I took a moment to stoke the fire in the fireplace. As I did so, it occurred to me that there were no lights outside in front of the cabin.

I didn't remember seeing a flashlight in my search for a sat phone, so I went about making a torch from a long sturdy piece of wood for the fireplace and my work shirt that I had arrived in. With a little lighter fluid, I would be ready to go.

I looked out the window and saw that most of the animals had withdrawn. It was getting dark, so I was glad to have made the torch.

I lit it in the fireplace and headed carefully out the door.

It was getting dark quickly and it was already starting to snow.

It would be a tricky drive in the icy dark back to town, but I was rather willing to risk it.

I held the torch in front of me and darted towards the car.

As I did so, the cougar leapt out from the darkness. It made a screeching sound as it flew through the air and landed near the car, directly in front of me.

I panicked and threw the torch at the green-eyed animal as I skidded to a stop. I turned and ran back into the cabin, slamming the door behind me.

I latched the door and went to the window above the little kitchen table to look out.

The cat sat casually by the torch, staring at me through the window with the eerie green glowing eyes.

I paced back and forth in the small cabin, trying to convince myself that this wasn't really happening.

I looked out the window and saw that the large cat had laid down next to the torch and made itself look rather comfortable. There didn't seem to be any fear of the fire at all in those glowing green eyes.

The snow started falling, delicately at first, and then harder and more adamantly as the night grew darker.

I stoked the fire and decided to wait it out.

The owner was supposed to meet me here the next day to pick up the key and the rest of the money I owed him. He drove a big truck with a radio in it. I would just have to wait it out.

I had food, water, and plenty of wood. And I was fairly sure that none of the animals could get into the cabin.

I just had to sit it out and wait until morning.

I tried to go about my evening, but I couldn't help looking outside periodically. The green eyes roamed the edge of the trees out in the darkness. One or two other animals dared to go and sit near the cat, so that they had a better view of the cabin.

I stoked the fire against the cold that was seeping in through the cracks and watched out the window almost obsessively.

The animals encroached closer and closer to the cabin. I checked all the doors and windows to make sure everything was locked and secure.

I laid down to try and get some sleep.

But it was no good. Any sleep I got would be fitful at best, and I kept getting up to check and see if the animals were still outside. I was hoping to maybe make a break for it out to the car.

But they seemed to stay close to the cabin, some occasionally falling to their sides and having what looked like small fits before awkwardly getting to their feet once again.

I could see their glowing eyes out in the darkness. The snow had stopped and some of the animals paced back and forth in front of the cabin.

I looked out the back windows as well, cupping my hand against the glass so I could see out into the darkness. More and more green eyes stared back at me.

When morning finally came, I was a mess. I was frazzled from too much coffee and a serious lack of sleep.

The animals had remained in their circle outside, keeping their nightlong vigil around the cabin.

I was relieved to see the sun finally rise, even though I was still trapped by the creatures. It wouldn't be too long before help arrived.

As I looked out into the early morning light, I could see that quite a few of the animals had fallen to the ground and laid there in the same mummified state as the deer I saw in my mad dash through the woods.

The cougar looked at me through the window and staggered to a standing position. It kept its eyes locked on the window as it lost its balance and fell over.

The black line that had formed on his back scattered slightly as the cat hit the ground and then the little black creatures huddled back together and started towards the cabin in a wave of chittering legs.

I grabbed my jacket and tried to stuff it under the door to keep them from crawling under it, but they were too small and too fast.

The tiny chittering creatures swarmed under the door and through cracks in the floor.

I tried to stomp on them as they came close, but they seemed to be exceptionally strong. They swarmed up my legs and I kicked and screamed and tried to brush them off.

There were too many and I couldn't get away from them.

They crawled up my body in an undulating swarm and then, after a searing pain pierced the base of my spine, I blacked out.

When the owner finally arrived at the cabin, there was nothing I could do.

I staggered to my feet when I heard him pull up outside.

He was screaming before I opened the door.

I watched my hand turn the knob and open the front door, and by the time I could get around to the driver's side of the truck, he had the nanites swarming all over him.

He reached out to me. But it was too late. For both of us.

I walked over to my car and opened the door. As I got into the driver's seat, my vision blinked in and out, like static on an old TV set.

A readout formed at the side of my vision.

In green glowing digital letters, I could read the ongoing process results of my body scan.

POTENTIAL ORGANIC FACTORY.

SCAN IN PROCESS...

RESULTS: OPTIMAL BIPEDAL ORGANIC FACTORY.

MINIMUM HEAT REQUIREMENTS MET.

I fought to keep my mind working. But the chittering was coming from the inside now.

I am Micah Adler. I am Micah Adler.

I kept repeating it to myself, so I wouldn't forget.

The pain in my spine was like a hot iron and my memories were fading as I drove back to the city. The chittering was taking control.

I am Micah Adl-

I am Mic-

I am.

I am Optimal Bipedal Organic Factory #0037.

I am to meet with the others in the city at 2100 hours.

What would you do if you discovered that your father was a reaper? And that your first step in following in his footsteps was one you didn't think you could make? Becoming a reaper can be much more personal than you might think.

The Reaper

When I woke up, it was like any other morning. Until it wasn't.

I had left my shade open again. It's how I've trained myself to rise with the sun. It works better in the warmer months, but it's better than waking up to the sound of some horrible electronic device. I just get to sleep in a little bit in the winter.

But electronic devices don't always work around me. I've never had the latest phone or computer. Mostly because there's just something about me that makes them not work reliably, so it's not worth the investment.

When the sun hits my eyes, I know it's time to wake up.

I throw the heavy blue quilt off myself and sit up. The room is unusually cold, and I shiver as the frigid air hits my body after the long hours hidden deep under the covers.

My black cat, Juliet, jumped into my lap as I rubbed my eyes and yawned. She seemed a little stressed out. She usually jumps on me when there's something going on that she doesn't like.

I rub her behind the ears, which usually calms her a bit, but instead she hissed at me and darted out of the room.

Crazy cat.

I stood up and stretched and reached for the hoodie that was on the chair at the foot of my bed. It was from my alma mater and was emblazoned with some ridiculous Valentine saying on it. I got it at an event my school had years ago. Not because of what the hoodie said on it, but because it was the softest and most comfortable thing I've ever worn in my life.

Cold mornings were meant for comfy hoodies and sweatpants.

I hit the bathroom and then headed towards the kitchen.

I could smell the enchanting scent of fresh brewed coffee.

I stopped in my tracks.

I stood frozen in place. I don't ever set my coffee maker to have coffee ready in the mornings. And I live alone. So as wonderful as the scent of fresh brewed coffee is in the morning, the fact that it was coming from my kitchen right now made me shiver harder than I had before I pulled on my hoodie.

I stood there for a few moments and listened. I could hear someone in the kitchen. I contemplated what I should do as I listened to cupboards being opened and closed and the sound of coffee being poured into a cup.

I started to slowly back up. I wanted to get back to my room and see if I could find some sort of a weapon. I was fairly certain I had a baseball bat somewhere in my closet.

Juliet came down the hall and sat in front of me and stared at me. From her vantage point, she could see into the kitchen, but I couldn't until I turned the corner. She looked back and forth from me to whoever was in there and looked at me like she was waiting for an introduction.

"I know you're there," a voice said from the kitchen. "I've already spoken to Juliet, she told me you were up."

The voice was half whisper half hiss, but it was loud enough that I could hear it clearly.

I slowly stepped forward and looked around the corner.

A tall figure in a dark cloak stood in the middle of my kitchen. I couldn't see his face under the hood, but he raised a cup of coffee to the dark space and took a tentative sip.

"You should buy better coffee," the hooded figure said. "It tastes better than this cheap crap. I can give you a recommendation if you'd like."

I stepped out to where the figure could see me and looked around the living room.

Candles were lit everywhere, giving the room an eerie glow. The blinds were all closed, so no early morning light had creeped into the room yet. The candles were all uncovered, the glass hurricane shields that I put over them were standing next to each one instead of over them.

"I like the cheap crap," I said. "Who the hell are you? And why are you dressed like Death?"

The figure laughed a deep creepy laugh.

"You're just like your mother," he said. "She liked the cheap crap too. And I'm not dressed like Death, he has much more style than this old thing."

He looked down at his cloak and then back up at me. He took another sip of his coffee.

"You knew my mother?" I asked.

The figure nodded and took another sip.

"So, if you're not Death," I started.

"I'm a reaper," he hissed. "But don't worry, I'm not here to take you. Not in the way you think anyway."

I looked down at my cat, who yawned and walked into the kitchen as if she was now bored with the intruder and wanted her breakfast.

"You need to come over here and have some coffee," the figure said. "We have a few things we need to talk about."

"No," I shook my head. "If you're not here to reap me, get out."

The hooded figure went over to the coffee maker and poured me a cup of coffee.

He held it out to me.

"Please," he said. "You have nothing to fear. Just come here and talk to me for a few minutes."

I forced my feet to move and I walked stiffly over to him. As I walked across the living room, each candle extinguished as I passed. I reached out and took the cup of coffee from his skeletal hand and joined him at my kitchen table.

He sat down across from me and pulled back his hood.

I gasped as I saw a creepy white skull with eyes still in their sockets.

"Oh sorry," he said. "I forgot."

He passed a bony hand over his face and then he turned into a man. He had dark curly hair like me and we had the same eyes, now that they were properly behind eyelids.

He looked like an older version of me.

"No," I said. "You're not-"

"Yes," he nodded. His hissing whisper of a voice became a normal man's voice, slightly deeper than my own, but strikingly similar. "I know your mother told you stories about your father."

"No," I said. "She said my father was in prison. That he was a killer."

"That was a half-truth, in a way, I guess." He shrugged, "I'm--"

"Don't say it," I stopped him.

"I have to," he said. "Your time has come to know the truth."

"There's no way," I felt a shiver crawling up my back.

My mother had told me terrible stories about my father. And none of them could possibly be true. None. No way. It was easier to believe that he was a murderer who died serving time in jail than the other stories.

"You know that I'm your father," he said. "I can see it in your eyes."

I could feel the anger burning in my chest.

I stood up so fast that my chair shot out behind me and hit the wall.

Juliet skittered out of the room and hid somewhere else in the house.

"You can't be," I said. "The stories she told me can't be true,"

"What, that your mother fell in love with a reaper?" he said.

"And now she's locked up in an asylum because everyone thinks she's crazy," I said.

"Yes, I know," he leaned back in the kitchen chair and took another sip of coffee. "It is much easier to visit her there."

"You visit--" I couldn't believe my ears.

I had always thought my mother was crazy. And now either I am too, or she's not.

At that moment, I didn't know which to believe.

The biggest problem was about to come.

I knew exactly what he was going to say next. She had told me, in her more lucid moments, that one day, my father would come for me.

"I'm here because it's time for you to join the family business," he said.

"Nope," I said. "Not gonna. No way."

"You have no choice in the matter," he said. "You are what you are, there's no avoiding it."

"No," I shook my head. "I have a choice. Everyone has a choice."

"Humans get choices," he looked at me sadly. "But tell me that you've never noticed that you're different."

I stood in the middle of my kitchen and thought about all the weird things in my life.

Electronics not working around me.

Curtains blow in an invisible wind when I walk past, which is why I only had shades and blinds in my house.

And this morning wasn't the first time that candles extinguished in my wake.

I've never been very popular at birthday parties.

But candles are more reliable than electric lights. They just have to be surrounded by glass. Which is why I have a lot of lanterns and hurricane lamps. And is why I was assuming he left the glass off the candles this morning. To help make his point.

"I need you to come with me today," he said.

"Why?" I asked.

"Because you need to see for yourself," he said.

"I'm not reaping anybody," I said. "I'm not going to become what you are."

"You already are," he said. "You just have to embrace it."

"No," I said.

"You have no choice in the matter," he said. "You are what you are."

I turned and started to walk out of the kitchen, but all of a sudden, instead of walking into my living room, I walked into a hospital room.

An old woman was lying in a hospital bed. She looked very small and old and frail. Like she had been wasting away for a while now. Her short silver hair was extremely thin, and I could see patches of her scalp in quite a few places. Despite her emaciated appearance, her wrinkled face looked rather peaceful.

She was hooked up to all sorts of beeping machines and tubes. On a chair next to her bed sat an old man that I could only assume was her husband. He held her frail white hand in his and he sat hunched towards her and was whispering softly to her.

"What are we doing here?" I asked him.

"We're doing what it is we do," he looked at me. "She will be your first."

I looked at the old woman lying in the bed.

"No," I shook my head.

"You need to see for yourself," he said.

"See what?" I asked.

"Talk to them," he pushed me forwards, into the room.

The old woman looked up at me and smiled.

"You're finally here," she said. "I've been waiting."

I looked back at him, the figure who stood behind me. He still looked like an older version of me, with his hood down and his brown curly hair showing. He nodded and gestured towards the old couple.

"Talk to them," he said.

"Do you know me?" I asked, slowly stepping forward.

She nodded and grinned at me. "You're here to release me from my pain."

I flashed a look back at him -- at my father -- and he gave me another nod.

I felt compelled to step forward and I could feel my arm wanting to reach out to her.

I forced my arms to stay at my sides and looked at the old man.

"Can he see me?" I asked the old woman.

She looked at her husband and smiled. She squeezed his hand as tight as her frail limb could manage and then looked back at me.

"No," she said. "But I know it's my time."

Her husband looked up at her face. "Who are you talking to?"

"They've come for me," she said to him. "My time has come."

"No," the old man shook his head. "You can't go without me. You can't leave me here alone. I love you too much to live without you."

She reached her other hand over to his and patted his hand. "It's my time."

The old man stood up and looked towards me -- and my father-- and pleaded with us desperately.

"Take me too," he said. "I can't go on without her. Please, take me with her."

He was looking desperately at us, but I could tell by his searching eyes that he couldn't see us. He was just looking where his wife had been looking.

I felt bad for the man. His wife was about to die and he was faced with living the last years of his life without her. I couldn't think of a more terrible fate.

I don't know what compelled me, but I reached out to him and placed my hand on his shoulder.

His eyes came to focus on me and he smiled with relief.

"So, you'll take me too?" He placed his hand on mine and gave my hand a squeeze like his wife had done to him.

I was startled. More startled than he was to suddenly see me.

What had I done?

I looked back to my father, and he was watching closely with an expressionless face.

He motioned for me to continue.

"I don't know if I can do that," I said.

"Please," the old man begged. "Please don't leave me here alone. I'm ready to go too. I'm 92 years old. We've been married for 70 years. Please, take me with her."

I don't know what compelled me, but I stepped forward and took the old woman's hand. I took his hand as well and then watched as the two of them faded.

It was like they paled into a glowing white. They both rose up into the air and smiled down at me.

"Thank you," they both said. "Thank you so much."

There was a small burst of white light, and they were gone.

I was suddenly startled back to reality as the old woman's machines started beeping furiously. Her heart monitor flatlined and several nurses rushed into the room. They ran right through me and over to the woman.

Her husband was slumped over with his head on her pillow next to hers and they both had the faintest hint of a smile on their faces.

I looked over at my father and he had a stunned look on his face.

"What?" I asked.

"It wasn't his time to go," my father said.

"Wait," I looked back at the bed where the nurses were desperately trying to deal with not one, but two bodies. "Was that wrong?"

"No," my father looked at me proudly. "You're a natural."

"How did that happen?' I asked. "I didn't mean for that to happen."

"But you did it," he said. "And you did it flawlessly."

"But you said it wasn't his time to go," I objected. "I shouldn't have taken him. There must be some kind of rule."

"He made his choice," my father said. "Some people are allowed that. If it truly wasn't his time, he could never have seen you."

"He made a choice?" I asked. "People can do that?"

"Only sometimes," he said. "And if they choose to live, they are on borrowed time."

"What happens on borrowed time?" I ask.

"You don't want to know," he said. "But that's one of the reasons I found you today. To discuss your options."

"And what option is that?" I asked. "You've already said this is what I am. That I have no choice in the matter. What exactly are my options?"

"Come and see," he said.

He turned and walked out of the hospital room and disappeared.

I followed him out and found myself someplace familiar.

It was the facility where my mother had lived for the last few years.

There were balloons taped to the wall and streamers floated in colorful loops around the rec room. Employees were setting places at a table and a few guests were being led in by a woman dressed in scrubs like a nurse.

"Looks like we made it just in time for a party," my father smiled.

"Who is the party for?" I asked.

"Don't know, don't care," he shrugged. "That's not why we're here."

He started out the door and headed down a light green hallway. The fluorescent lights in the ceiling above us flickered as we walked under each one, giving the hallway a creepy and ominous feeling.

"Where are we going?" I asked.

"That's right," he said softly. "You would have never been back this way."

"Why are you whispering," I asked. "If no one can see us?"

"I can hear you," a man said from inside his room. "I could feel you both coming."

"Who was that?" I asked.

"You have to be careful in places like this," my father said. "You can be seen and heard by people who drift between worlds, even if it's not their time."

"Lovely," I said.

"You've never seen your mother's room, have you?" he asked.

"No," I said. "When I visit, they have us sit in the rec room. Or sometimes they let us go for a walk outside."

A thought just occurred to me.

"She shouldn't be here, should she?"

My heart sank in my chest as I realized that all of the stories my mother told me were probably true. She wasn't insane. She was right. And she just happened to see things other people didn't and didn't know better than to keep quiet about it.

She had spent the last few years of her life in a hospital where she didn't need to be. Probably taking loads of medication that she didn't need. All because she could see my father.

We walked through a door, no need to open it, and my mother was sitting on a neatly made-up bed, staring out the window at a small brown bird that was singing in the tree that shaded her room from the outside. The room was sparse, but comfortable looking. More comfortable than I imagined it would be in a place like this.

"I brought someone to see you," my father said.

My mother turned to look at us and her eyes widened in recognition.

"I see you've started him along his path," she said calmly.

"Mom," I started towards her and then stopped.

"I don't think I can hug you anymore," I said.

"Nonsense," she stood up and walked over and pulled me into a tight hug. "My boy can always hug his mother."

"But shouldn't my touch kill you?" I asked.

"Only if I take your hand," she said. "And you're not killing anyone, you know. You are helping them move on."

"I've started teaching him the ropes this morning," my father said.

He went over and gave my mother a hug and a kiss.

I wasn't sure if I should be happy to see my parents together or be revulsed for a myriad of reasons.

She looked at me and then back to my father.

"How's he doing?" she asked.

She asked the question like it was any other job that my father was teaching me. Not reaping. Not taking lives. But just an occupation that I was now in training for, with my long-lost father as my new killing mentor.

"He's already done his first reaping," he said proudly. "It was a double. Took an old man with his sick wife."

"That's very good for a first time," she looked at me and smiled widely. "I'm very proud of you."

"Are you kidding me?" Maybe she should be here. She thought that what I had done earlier that morning was a good thing. Ending someone's life before it was their time did not seem like something to be celebrating.

"I can't believe all of your stories were true," I said. "I am so sorry."

"There's nothing to be sorry about," she said. "But I'm so glad you're here. That it's going to be you."

"What's going to be me?" I asked.

I looked back and forth between my mother and father.

"Why did you bring me here?" I demanded.

"As I have already told you, those that can see a reaper and choose to live are only living on borrowed time," my father said.

I stared at my father and let that sink in for a moment. I looked over at my mother.

"You're on--" I couldn't bring myself to say it.

"Borrowed time," she said. "You can say it. It's all right. It's not like I don't already know."

"But how, or why?" I asked.

"I was in a car accident," she said. "Before I had you. When your father showed up to reap me, he stayed with me until the ambulance came instead. He rode with me to the hospital, and he stayed with me the whole time I was there."

"But why?" I asked.

"Haven't you ever heard of love at first sight?" my father asked. "I couldn't reap her. I had fallen in love."

"So, for my whole life, you've been on borrowed time?" I asked.

They both nodded.

"What does that mean?" I asked.

"The longer a person lives on borrowed time, the larger their chances are of going to a not so nice place after they are finally reaped," my mother said. "That's why your father brought you here."

"Wait, because you've been on borrowed time for almost 30 years, you're going to go to hell?" I asked.

"It is only absolute if your father is the one who reaps me," she said.

"I don't understand," I looked at my father.

"Your mother agreed to come here because she was being hunted by other reapers. But they have found her again," my father said. "And they're not happy that she has avoided death for so long."

"So, they want to send her to hell too?" I asked.

"In a manner of speaking, yes," she said.

"Why am I here?" I stared at them in disbelief.

"Because the one who finally reaps her gets to make the choice," my father said.

"What choice?" I asked.

"You get to choose what happens to your mother," he said. "You're the only reaper we can trust with the job."

"You brought me here to reap my own mother?" I couldn't hide my astonishment.

"I can't do it," my father said. "And if one of the others does, then your mother is doomed."

"You can't be serious," I stared at my mother.

She held her hands out to me.

"I would rather have it be you," she said. "So I can go on to a better place."

"I can't," I put my hands behind my back. "I can't kill my own mother."

"It's not killing," she reminded me. "My time was up long ago. I need you to rescue me from a terrible fate. You're the only one I can trust."

I stared at my father.

"The others are coming," he said.

He nodded towards the door.

I could hear the cries of the man who could hear us in the hallway calling out to someone to take him as well.

"You have to take me," my mother pleaded. "There's no more time."

She reached out to me, fingers splayed wide, shaking her hands in a desperate motion.

A hooded figure stepped through the door and laughed when he saw us all.

"She's mine," he said in a hissing voice.

"No," I leaped out and grabbed my mother by the hands. "I'm sorry. I am so so sorry."

"Don't be sorry," she said as she started to fade into the white light. "I love you."

"I love you too, Mom," I said.

She disappeared in a burst of white light and left me and my father and the other reaper standing alone in her room.

My mother's body was on her bed. She looked like she had just fallen over from where she had been sitting while watching the bird. She looked like she had a content smile on her face.

"Who are you?" the reaper looked at me.

"I'm new," I stammered.

"He's my son," my father said, proudly standing next to me.

The reaper turned and looked at me with his faceless hood.

"Damn nepotism," he muttered. He turned and disappeared through the door.

I turned back to look at my mother's body.

"I just reaped my own mother," I said softly.

"It was far past her time to go," my father put his arm around me. "You saved her from a terrible place. You should be proud."

"I'm not proud," I said. "I can't do this."

"Yes, you can," my father smiled. "You did something that I never could. Like I said. You're a natural."

Not everyone knows when they have a haunted house on their street. Not even those who live there. This is another story that starts with a young child and a dog. Don't worry, they will be all right.

Visitors

Mrs. Lewis looked out the front window and saw a small child walking down the street alongside a black Giant Schnauzer. She frowned through her lace curtains and walked over to the window to get a better look. She pulled back the delicate white lace that shielded her living room from the afternoon sun and squinted over her reading glasses to get a better look.

"George," she called out.

George was sitting in his chair in the living room reading the newspaper and smoking his pipe. He was in the same room with his wife, so he didn't see any need for her to bellow his name as loudly as she had.

"I'm right here," he said. "You don't have to yell."

"There's a little boy wandering around alone outside in the street," she said. "I don't see his mother anywhere."

George put down his newspaper, knowing that this was the type of situation he needed to address, or else he would never get any reading done. He set his pipe down in the holder that he kept on the table next to his chair.

He stood up and walked over to the window and looked out over his wife's shoulder. They had been married for over 60 years, so he knew he needed to look or she would pester him to death until he did.

"He's not alone," George said. "He's got a big dog with him."

The dog was huge. It was a Giant Schnauzer that outweighed the child by two or three times at least. He walked at a slow pace so that the little boy could keep his balance by resting his grubby little hand on the dog's back as they walked.

"Who would let their toddler walk a dog that big?" His wife asked.

"I'm sure his mother is somewhere close by," George said.

"Should we call someone?" she asked.

George sat back down in his chair and picked up his newspaper again. "Who exactly are you going to call, Loretta?"

His wife went over to the front door and set her hand on the knob.

"Well, then," she said. "I'm going to go outside and ask him where he lives. Maybe I can take him home."

"Go right ahead," George said as he rustled his newspaper and settled back into the chair to read.

Loretta walked over to the front door and tried to open it. She tried the knob and it wouldn't budge.

"George," she said. "This darn doorknob is stuck again."

"I'll fix it," George said through taking a puff on his pipe.

He continued to scan the sports section without getting up.

Loretta went back to the front window and looked out again.

"Where did they go?" she asked.

George looked up to see his wife kneeling on the couch and straining to look out the window.

"They probably went home," George said.

Loretta went back to the front door and tried the knob again.

"I really wish you would fix this," she muttered to George.

"I'll get right on it, dear," George said.

*

Loretta was in the kitchen a little while later making lunch.

She was standing over the stove making George's favorite. Grilled cheese, ham, and tomato sandwiches. She had whipped up some cream of broccoli soup to go with it and was just finishing as she heard an old but familiar noise.

The old doggie door on the back door next to the kitchen opened and closed. The flap clicked behind whatever had come in through the little door.

"George," she called to him from the kitchen. "We've got raccoons again. Will you nail that dog door shut please?"

"I'll get to it when I fix the doorknob," he called back from the living room.

Loretta sighed and went over and grabbed a broom. She went to the backdoor and gasped when she saw what had come through into her mudroom.

The little boy from the street was standing up from crawling his way through the dog door and he straightened up and looked around the mudroom.

His wide brown eyes took in all the sights around him and he gasped slightly when his dog squeezed through the too small dog door behind him.

Loretta stood staring at the two invaders with the broom still in her hand.

The dog stood up to his full height and sniffed the air. The black Giant Schnauzer easily came up to her waist and he looked around protectively. The child grabbed at the dog to help his balance and the two stood looking around. Their eyes fixed on the doorway where Loretta stood.

"George?" she said. "We might have a problem."

George got up from his chair in the living room and came into the kitchen. He walked over the smooth kitchen tile and looked over his wife's shoulder to see what she was looking at.

"You going to hit them with that?" George asked, seeing that his wife was holding a broom out in front of her.

"I don't know what to do," she said. "Why are they here?"

"Who knows?" George said. "My guess is that they were just exploring and found Rex's old door."

"So, after they leave, you're going to fix the dog door, right?" Loretta asked as she watched her husband walk over to the pot of soup that was steaming on the stove.

"I'll get to it," he said.

George stood over the food on the stove and breathed deeply. "I sure do miss the smell of cream of broccoli soup and grilled ham sandwiches. You hardly make them anymore."

"I make them every single day," Loretta turned and looked at him. "It seems like it's all we ever eat."

George looked back over at the dog and snorted out a laugh. "I'm surprised that dog isn't over here with me."

"Maybe he doesn't like broccoli," Loretta said.

She eyed the dog as he entered the kitchen and sniffed around the room. The dog sneezed and it almost knocked the boy who was clinging to the hair on the dog's side for balance.

"I think that's the boy from two doors down," George said. "Doesn't he look like his mother?"

Loretta took a good look at the boy. "He does look a bit like Nancy," she agreed. "I wonder if she even knows he's gone."

"Since when do they have a dog?" George asked.

"They've had the dog longer than they've had the boy," Loretta said. She squinted at the dog's collar.

"Bucky?" she read.

The dog's head snapped to look directly at her.

"Hi, there, Bucky," Loretta said. "Good doggie."

She reached towards the dog and it let out an eardrum shattering deep bark.

"I wouldn't mess with the dog," George said. "That's a protective breed."

"Bucky?" a voice called from outside. "Bucky? Are you in there?"

Loretta looked out the window. "It's Nancy," she sighed with relief. "I'm glad. This boy shouldn't be out alone. Even with the monstrous dog protecting him."

The dog door lifted and Nancy's face could be seen through the hole in the door.

"Carter!" The woman's voice was filled with relief. "Bucky, you bring Carter to me right now."

The dog obediently walked to the dog door and sniffed through the hole at the woman.

"You two know better than to go outside without permission," Nancy said.

The woman reached through the dog door and up to the lock on the back door. She undid the deadbolt and opened the door.

The door swung open and she rushed in to pick up her son.

"Carter," she pulled the child up into her arms and hugged him tightly. "How did the two of you get out?"

She looked at the boy in her arms and he just giggled.

"Bucky," she looked down at the dog. "I don't know if I should thank you or scold you."

"The dog is very protective of the boy," George said. "You should be proud."

Nancy looked around the kitchen.

"I can't believe you got in here," she said. "We'd better talk to the Homeowner's Association about having that dog door boarded up. It's not safe for you or other kids to be wandering around in an abandoned house like this."

George and Loretta looked at one another.

"Poor old Loretta," Nancy said. "It's a shame what happened here."

She looked at her son and took the dog by the collar. "Let's go home," Nancy said. "This old place gives me the creeps."

The three left out the back door and headed home.

"What did she mean?" Loretta asked.

George eyed his wife and shrugged, "Darned if I know."

Loretta handed George the broom and turned back to the stove to finish tending to lunch.

George glanced over at the axe by the backdoor and placed the broom in front of it to hide the axe. And his shame.

*This series was started shortly after the death of my older brother. I wrote it for him. Here is **The Wild Hunt** in its entirety.*
Eli dreams of living in a fantasy world where he is a warrior and a leader. But in reality, he just works in retail. Until one night...

Aeris Awakens

Elijah muttered to himself as he slammed his shovel into the loosely packed snow over and over again.

He hated snow. The white featureless landscape it created. The frigid cold that made his fingers hurt, even through the warm black gloves his mom had sent him last Christmas.

He missed living where there was no snow in the winter. Where it was warmer and there was no shoveling every morning for months.

He shoveled pile after pile out of the driveway. His back had started to hurt and his arms already ached after only a few minutes. He scanned the driveway and the distance to the street.

Laziness won out and he gave up. He'd rather walk to work than continue shoveling. Elijah convinced himself that it wasn't that far.

He tossed the shovel back into the garage where it landed in the corner with a satisfying clang and fell to the floor, taking a rake and a broom with it. The clatter was loud and it probably could be heard by the neighbors. He didn't care. It was his garage. He could do what he wanted.

He stomped the snow off himself and went back inside to change into work clothes and dry boots.

Eli stood at his closet and looked at the contents. He grabbed the blue collared polo shirt required for his job and pulled it on. He kept his work shirts next to his cosplay garb. Next to what he'd rather be wearing.

The green leather armor hung unfinished in the closet and made him drift off into another world for a moment. A world where he was a hunter. A warrior. An elf ranger that had adventures and made his own decisions. Not someone who had to work in an electronics store to pay his half of the rent on a crappy apartment in a small tourist town.

Eli finished dressing and headed outside. Back into the frigid cold and the blinding white snow.

He trudged through the snow to work. He trudged through his day at the retail electronics store where he catered to snotty entitled tourists who had lost their phone chargers and headphones. His mind wandered throughout the day back to what he wished he could be. A warrior, free to roam the countryside. Saving village people from monsters and maidens from villains.

At the end of the day, he set back out into the freezing cold to trudge his way back home. Just so he could do it all again tomorrow.

He decided to take a shortcut through the woods that led to a clearing behind his apartment building. The risk of running into a bear was low this time of year. But he could let his mind wander again, to the life he wished he had.

He listened to the crunch of the snow beneath his boots with each step and breathed in the smell of the snow. People had argued with him that snow was just frozen water, and it didn't have a scent and that what he was smelling was a lack of smells, dampened by the snow itself.

But Eli disagreed. It smelled like calm.

The one time he liked the snow was at night. When it was quiet. When he didn't have to go to work. When he could enjoy the fact that he didn't have to be anywhere or do anything.

He crunched along in the moonlight, thinking about the fact that all he had to do tonight was make some dinner and play video games for the rest of the night. The only place he could live his dream.

He had leftover pizza waiting for him in the fridge and a scheduled game online with his friends. His 80th level character was waiting, patiently, for him to come back. His idea of a perfect evening.

As he went deeper into the woods, he saw something flicker past in his peripheral vision.

He turned to see a shadow ducking behind some trees a bit in the distance.

"Hello?" he stopped and called out to the shadow.

Everything stayed quiet. Almost too quiet. Eli couldn't remember the forest ever being so still before, even on a winter night.

"Is someone there?" Eli took a few steps toward the direction he thought the shadow had gone.

There was a clearing in the treetops, just large enough so he could see past the tall pines and view the sky above him. He looked up into the full moonlight and saw a large group of creatures running through the sky. Some looked like they could be men, others definitely weren't. It was an enormous and noisy charge that filled the sky and momentarily blocked out the moonlight. They raced across the view allowed by the treetops and out of sight. Eli could still hear the faint yelling of the charge ringing in his ears and trailing off into the distance.

He heard a twig crack in the trees and turned his head to see a form taking advantage of his lack of attention and making a run for it.

"Stop," Eli called out. "Wait."

Eli started through the snow and followed the shadowy figure through the forest.

Eli knew the forest well and took a turn to cut the shadowy figure off before it could escape deeper into the woods.

The trees flashed by as Eli closed in on his prey.

He grew close enough to reach out and grab the tunic of the person he was pursuing.

"Stop," Eli shouted.

His fingers caught in the rough fabric just enough to pull the man off balance and both of them went tumbling through the cold, wet snow.

The figure recovered quickly and tried to scramble off, but Eli recovered also and grabbed the shadowy figure by the foot.

"Stop," Eli said. "I'm not going to hurt you."

The figure whipped around and faced Eli in the moonlight.

"But I may just hurt you," it hissed.

Eli gasped as he saw the creature for the first time. It definitely wasn't human.

He had deep blue, almost purplish skin and his eyes glowed yellow in the darkness. He was wispy thin and lanky and extremely tall.

They both scrambled to their feet and Eli stood in front of the creature, who towered at least a full head taller than Eli. He had long black hair that was in thin braids that reached all the way to his waist.

The creature was wearing black leather armor that made him look like a shadow, even in the full moonlight.

"Nice armor," Eli whispered.

The creature pulled a sword from beneath his dark cape and placed it under Eli's chin before Eli had a chance to move.

"Who are you?" the creature asked.

"What are you?" Eli responded.

The creature sighed, annoyed.

"I am a night elf, you doltish human," he growled. "And you will die here tonight if you don't answer my questions."

"Right," Eli said. "I am E-"

Eli stopped. He thought this couldn't be real. He must be dreaming.

Night elves were something of video games and role-playing games, not real life.

But if this *was* real...

Eli racked his brain.

Never give a fae your real name.

"My name is Aeris Jagger," Eli gave the name of one of his video game characters. "I am the leader of the elf rangers of the forest."

The night elf tilted his head to one side and checked Eli's ears.

"You are not an elf, human," the night elf said. "You're lying, I can smell it."

"I didn't say I was an elf," Eli stammered slightly. "I said I was their leader."

The night elf narrowed his eyes at Eli.

"You are a leader of elves," the night elf scoffed. Eli nodded.

"Then prove it," the night elf said.

"Prove it?" Eli asked. "How?"

"Summon your elves," the night elf said, brandishing his sword in the moonlight. "*Leader*."

"They're out on a mission," Eli said.

"Liar," the night elf scoffed.

"I'm not lying," Eli insisted.

"If you are a leader of elves," the night elf said. "Then you must be a master of weapons. You must join me on the Wild Hunt."

"What's the Wild Hunt?" Eli asked.

The night elf lowered his sword and stepped towards Eli. He pivoted slightly and gestured to the sky, "You saw the hunting party, running across the sky?"

Eli nodded, "Yes."

"That is the Wild Hunt," he said.

"Who were they?" Eli asked.

The night elf looked at him, amused, "They are the fae, the undead, and any creature that wants to join in on the hunt."

"What are they hunting?" Eli asked.

The night elf grinned, "You must come and find out for yourself."

Eli shook his head, "I don't think so."

"You, Aeris Jagger, have no choice but to join," the night elf said. "For anyone who has witnessed the Wild Hunt must join or die."

"Technically, that is a choice," Eli said.

The night elf turned faster than Eli could react and Eli felt the cold edge of the sword resting under his chin again.

"What is your choice, Aeris Jagger, leader of the elf rangers?" the night elf stared at Eli across the blade shimmering in the moonlight with his cold yellow eyes. They looked like a cat's eyes, with the black pupil wide in the darkness.

Eli felt a surge of bravery and he reached up and pushed the sword blade away from his chin with one carefully placed finger.

"I'll join," Eli said. "But I am not dressed for a hunt."

The night elf looked him up and down and turned towards the forest where he had been hiding, "Follow me."

*

Eli followed the night elf through the dark woods.

He had to almost jog because the night elf had much longer legs than he did, and his pace was quick. Eli didn't have time to listen to and enjoy the crunch of his boots in the snow, but he did notice that he was suddenly no longer in familiar territory.

He was in the woods, but they weren't his woods. It wasn't the woods near his home, where he knew the area well.

The trees were taller, denser. The woods were darker. Even with the full moon flickering in and out of the sky through the treetops that towered above them.

Eli felt like he was being watched. From everywhere. He couldn't shake the feeling that there were eyes on his constantly. And he could hear faint whispers among the trees as he passed.

As they made their way through the forest, Eli could feel his gait change. He looked down to see that he was wearing his green leather armor.

Not the pieced together armor that hung in his closet, waiting to be finished. It was the armor he dreamed of, that imaginary outcome that he wished he could create.

It had everything that he had imagined, down to the last detail.

The fur-lined cowl, the dark wool cape with highly detailed Celtic knots forged into the plate shoulder guards. The cape was heavy, but glided across the top of the snow with ease, keeping him surprisingly warm.

He had Celtic knotted metal wrist guards, fitted perfectly over heavy leather gloves. His hands felt warmer than they had in the gloves his mother had given him.

The lightweight green body armor that he had always imagined fit so well that it looked like clothing rather than armor. He almost tripped when he was trying to admire the quality and the fit while still trying to keep up with the night elf.

"Where are we going?" Eli asked, trying not to sound as winded as he felt.

His heavy leather boots with buckles and shin guards looked cool, but were getting heavier with every step.

"You'll see when we get there," the night elf said.

Strapped to his back, Eli could feel a longbow and a quiver of arrows. A sword dangled in a sheath on each side of his belt, and knives were hidden in all of the places he had imagined being able to hide a knife.

"Can you at least tell me your name?" Eli asked.

He could move surprisingly easily. Only occasionally getting poked or smacked by something hidden in his belt or boot or folds of his cape. He was just not used to the weight of the clothing. Leather and wool were heavy, not to mention the metal guards.

"You can call me Sagewalker," the night elf said.

"Sagewalker?" Eli repeated, trying to hide a laugh.

The night elf stopped and turned to face Eli, "Do you have a problem with my name?"

Eli stopped, and looked up at the night elf and into his creepy yellow eyes.

"No, none at all," Eli said. "I just repeat names so I don't forget them."

Sagewalker grunted and turned back to his path.

Eli continued to follow him.

"How much farther is it?" Eli asked.

Sagewalker turned and glared at him, "Do you talk this much with the day elves?"

"They tend to be," Eli paused slightly. "Friendlier."

"Not the ones I've met," Sagewalker growled.

Eli stood and stared at the night elf. He still couldn't believe this was real. He was waiting to wake up. To realize that all this had only been a dream.

But his face was too cold and his nose was running from the frigid night air. His nose was never runny and his face never hurt in his dreams.

He continued to follow the night elf for what seemed like it should be a long way. But they never seemed to get anywhere. Eli felt like they were passing the same landmarks over and over again.

"Are we going in circles?" Eli asked.

The night elf grinned back at him.

"You've passed the first test," Sagewalker said.

Eli stopped walking. "This was a test?"

"Yes," Sagewalker said. "It took you long enough, but you passed."

"I can't believe it," Eli stammered. "If I knew this was going to be a test."

"What?" Sagewalker mocked. "You would've studied?"

"I would've paid attention more," Eli said. "I thought you were just leading me somewhere."

"Always assume everything is a test," Sagewalker said. "Or at least don't blindly trust a stranger who is leading you somewhere unknown."

Eli just glared at him.

"Silly human," Sagewalker turned back to the path and started walking again.

"So, are we in phase two now?" Eli asked as he started following the night elf. "Are we starting the second test? Because this time, I'm ready."

Sagewalker laughed and kept walking.

Eli followed in silence. He was getting tired and this wasn't feeling like an adventure anymore. It felt like a hike. In weather that was too cold with a leader he didn't want to follow anymore.

The night was getting darker and colder and later, although the moon was still lighting the way as it moved across the sky.

When Eli finally felt like he just wanted to turn back, he heard something off in the distance.

"What is that?" Eli asked.

"Shhh," Sagewalker waved him to silence.

The two quietly ran over and hid behind some bushes and Sagewalker pointed to a clearing ahead of them.

"Watch," he whispered.

Eli focused his eyes on the clearing. His eyelids were feeling heavy and he was growing more and more tired. But he watched the clearing and waited.

The sounds were getting closer. It sounded like hundreds of voices and hooves beating on the ground. A crowd stampeding closer and closer. The ground started to feel like it was shaking beneath him.

As he watched the clearing, creatures of all sorts ran into sight. Hellhounds led the charge, barking and howling as they led the pack into the clearing. There were centaurs with their bows drawn and more night elves than he could count. There were all manner of creatures that Eli couldn't even identify. All were armed and all looked like they were chasing something. Hunting something. Ready to kill something.

The hellhounds screeched to a halt. Their jagged toothed mouths dripping slobber and blood. They had very little hair, but their bodies were tightly wound muscles, ready to pounce as soon as they caught wind of their prey.

Eli tried to remain quiet. He didn't even want to breathe for fear of the hellhounds catching his scent.

"Are you ready?" Sagewalker whispered.

"Ready for what?" Eli whispered back.

"To join the hunt," Sagewalker said.

"No," Eli changed his mind. "I'm good."

"It is join or die," Sagewalker said. "I will kill you right here in hiding, like the coward you are."

Eli sighed. "Whatever."

Sagewalker grinned at him, his yellow cat-like eyes gleaming in the moonlight. Eli suddenly felt like he should have never trusted the night elf.

Sagewalker grabbed Eli before he could react and twisted his arm behind his back. Sagewalker dragged Eli to his feet and pushed him out in front of him like a shield as he walked towards the armed and battle-ready crowd.

Eli watched in horror as the hellhounds locked their eyes on him and growled menacingly.

"My fellow huntsmen," Sagewalker yelled. "I have found my surety."

The entire hunting party was now staring at them. Sagewalker continued to hold Eli tightly in front of him. His grip was like iron and no matter what Eli did, he couldn't shake the night elf's grasp.

"What?" Eli said. "What's a surety?"

The hunting party made room for a man - a creature - that looked like something undead. He was extremely tall, dwarfing the centaurs as he passed them. His wrinkled and rotting skin was tinted a light blue in the moonlight and he was wearing animal furs over his leather and iron clad armor. He had an ax with a long handle and carried it like he was ready to swing it at any time. And he wore a crown on his head that looked like it was made of bones and ice.

His cold eyes felt like they were boring a hole through Eli.

Eli found it difficult to meet the creature's gaze.

"What is your name?" the creature said.

Eli tried to speak, but no words came.

"He said his name is Aeris Jagger," Sagewalker said.

The creature looked at Eli as if he were analyzing him. "He lies."

"He said he was the leader of elven rangers," Sagewalker said.

Eli felt himself grow colder with each step the creature took towards him. A cold that felt like it would never leave him. His bones felt like they were being covered with frost and he started to shiver uncontrollably in the creature's presence.

It only took the creature a few of his long-legged steps and he was in front of Eli, staring down at him.

Sagewalker loosened his grip on Eli.

"No one lies to me," the creature said.

"I-I was afraid to give a fae my real name," Eli stammered.

The creature chuckled, "You're smarter than you look."

"I-I also didn't agree to be a surety," Eli said.

"No one agrees to be a surety," the creature laughed. "You just are one."

"What?" Eli gasped. "Why?"

"Sagewalker was banded as a traitor," the creature said. "Killed one of our own."

"Accidentally," Sagewalker chimed in.

"There are no accidents," the creature snapped at the night elf.

He looked back to Eli, "His punishment was death, or bringing in a new quarry."

"That would be you," Sagewalker whispered over Eli's shoulder.

"Quarry?" Eli looked over at the crowd of hunters, who were staring at him like he was lunch and they hadn't eaten in days.

"I'm not quarry," Eli said. "I'm no one's quarry."

Eli reached back into his belt with his free hand and pulled a knife out from behind him. He pivoted around before the night elf knew what was happening and stabbed Sagewalker in the neck.

More blood than Eli ever expected spattered out onto the white snow. He stepped away and watched as Sagewalker fell lifeless between him and the ice creature.

Eli looked up at the creature in front of him. When he met the creature's eyes, it started to laugh.

Eli drew his swords. He knew it was futile, but the adrenaline coursing through his veins decided he wasn't going down without a fight.

"Hold," the creature put up a hand to stop Eli.

Eli stood in the snow, with the night elf still bleeding into the snow at his feet. His shivering had become almost violent, but he did all he could to stand his ground.

The creature grinned at Eli, "You have earned your way into the hunt."

"I'm no one's quarry," Eli almost shouted.

"No, you're certainly not," the creature said. "You are one of us now."

"What?" Eli said.

"There is no escape but death," the creature said to Eli. "You join the hunt, forever more, or you will freeze to death where you stand."

Eli could feel himself starting to succumb to the cold. He looked over at the hunting party in desperation. They stood in silence, waiting for his decision.

"Okay," Eli relented. "I'll join."

The creature held out his ax and touched Eli on each shoulder, "You will forevermore be Aeris Jagger, leader of the elf rangers, and member of the Wild Hunt."

Eli suddenly felt the cold melting away from his bones. He felt warmer, stronger.

He reached up to feel his ears, which had grown larger and to a point. His hearing was much better than he ever thought it could be. His vision sharper. And his sense of smell had heightened, much to his dismay.

"You can never return to your world," the creature said to him. "You are one of us now."

Eli looked down at the night elf, who was fading away into the snow, as if he never had been.

"Come, Aeris," the creature led him to the cheering party. "Tonight, we hunt."

Aeris returns to track down his memories. But finds something else entirely. -- Follow up short story to Aeris Awakens. Part 2 of The Wild Hunt.

Aeris Redeemed

I am Aeris Jagger, leader of the elf rangers, member of the Wild Hunt.

Aeris pondered this on many nights, while hiding in the shadows, like there was something missing. Something he had forgotten. It felt like the memory was still there, just waiting to be found, but as soon as he got close to it, it drifted away and evaporated like his breath in the cold.

My first kill was Sagewalker, the night elf. A traitor.

Aeris couldn't remember why Sagewalker was a traitor. What was it that he had done?

Why had Aeris been so willing to kill him?

Aeris smelled the frigid night air. It had been winter for as long as he could remember. The fresh snow covered so many scents. To Aeris, snow smelled like… calm.

It was deathly quiet. Even his elf ears couldn't hear much more than the snowflakes falling to the earth.

All was still, but the Hunt was still on.

The Hunt was always on.

Aeris waited. He looked across the empty meadow, covered with a blanket of pristine white snow. Dothar, another member of the Hunt, was on the other side. They had both been sent to scout the meadow, and what might be hiding on the other side.

They had been scouting side by side for what seemed like forever, although Aeris knew that couldn't be true. Dothar used to be human at some point. He had close cropped hair and a scruff of a beard. His facial scars told of many battles, even though Dothar himself never spoke of them.

Dothar signaled to Aeris to move forward.

He silently obeyed. But Aeris felt like no matter how long they searched, they would never find their prey.

Night after night, they hunted. Aeris didn't even know how large the hunting party was. Every night they hunted, forever searching for something that eluded them. Just like that thought that he couldn't get out of his mind. Or find.

There was something else. Something he needed to remember.

And there was nothing on the other side of the meadow. That he suddenly knew for a fact.

Aeris stood up. Dothar signaled for him to get down again.

Aeris was tired of crouching in the cold. He was tired of trying to move stealthily through the fresh snow. He was tired of the hunt.

Aeris walked out to the center of the meadow. He looked up at the night sky and stared at the full moon that had been rising above them. It was their only light, but it was enough for his elven eyes.

He sheathed his sword, which he had been carrying by his side. He walked down the center of the meadow empty handed, Dothar desperately trying to get his attention without making noise.

It was too late, if there was something there, it already knew that Aeris was there too.

He walked boldly, but still somewhat quietly, through the snow. He was an elf after all. Walking quietly just happened naturally. The snow was ankle-deep to his boots and his wool cape dragged across the cold wet footprints that he left behind him.

He listened to his boots crunching through the snow. He was surprised that he was making any sound with his steps. He found the noise comforting. Like it was something familiar from childhood, but he couldn't place it.

Dothar was pacing him, but remained silent and hidden in the shadows of the trees on the edge of the meadow.

"Come out, Dothar," Aeris called out into the silence. "There's nothing here."

There was a pause. Then Dothar appeared at the edge of the meadow.

His friend was bathed in the soft moonlight and looked angry.

"What do you think you're doing?" Dothar asked.

"There's nothing out there," Aeris said.

He gestured towards the direction they were heading, "We are following nothing." Aeris said. "We're wasting our time."

"We're scouts," Dothar said. "We're supposed to find something."

"There is nothing out there," Aeris insisted.

"Then we should try somewhere else," Dothar looked around. "Which direction should we go?"

"Have you ever caught anything?" Aeris asked.

"What?" Dothar turned his attention back to Aeris. "What do you mean?"

"Have you ever caught your prey?" Aeris asked. "In all your time in the Wild Hunt, have you ever caught anything?"

Dothar thought for a moment, "We must have. We're still alive, aren't we?"

"Being alive has nothing to do with whether or not we've ever caught our prey," Aeris said.

"We must have eaten something," Dothar was starting to sound confused. "We must have caught something."

"Do you remember the last time you've eaten?" Aeris asked.

Dothar stared at Aeris, "No, but I don't feel hungry either."

"Neither do I," Aeris said. "Doesn't that seem weird to you? We can't remember catching or eating anything? Ever?"

Dothar stared at the meadow around them. There was no sign of life. Just white snow-covered shapes of bushes and trees and the ground blanketed with snow. Their own footprints being the only sign of life.

"What do you think it means?" Dothar asked after a pause.

"I think we're being punished," Aeris said.

"For what?" Dothar asked. "What have we done?"

"I don't know," Aeris said. "I can't remember anything before joining the hunt. Can you?"

"I joined the hunt years ago," Dothar said. "It has been my whole life."

"That's my point," Aeris said. "Can you remember anything before the hunt? Anything? From your childhood, perhaps?"

Dothar thought for a few moments more. He scrunched up his forehead and stared at the ground, as if he were searching the ground for any memories that may have fallen onto it like the snow.

"I can't remember anything," Dothar said. "Nothing. No childhood. No mother, no father. Nothing before joining the hunt."

"I can't either," Aeris said. "I keep thinking there is something I've forgotten, but I can't reach it. I can't find it. It's like it's been erased from my memory."

Dothar stared at Aeris, "What do we do?"

Aeris shrugged, "Find answers?"

"How?" Dothar asked. "No one is going to have our memories for us."

"Maybe not," Aeris said. "But what if there is?"

"Is what?" Dothar asked.

"What if there is someone who is a keeper of memories?" Aeris said.

"That would be sorcery," Dothar said.

"Then we need to find a sorcerer," Aeris said.

"There are no sorcerers in the hunt," Dothar said. "Contact with the outside world is forbidden."

"Why?" Aeris asked.

"Why what?" Dothar didn't understand the question.

"Why is contact with the outside world forbidden?" Aeris asked.

Dothar thought for a moment. "I don't know."

"I'm going to find a sorcerer," Aeris said. "I don't care what the rules say."

"Then you will be branded as a traitor and hunted," Dothar said.

"Then let them hunt me," Aeris said.

Dothar drew his sword.

Aeris sighed and faced his friend. They had known each other as long as Aeris could remember. Even though he couldn't remember how long that was. They were friends. At least he thought they were something like friends. Aeris did not want to face off against his friend.

"Don't do this," Aeris said.

"I have to," Dothar said. "You know the rules. They will hunt you. And if I just let you go; they will hunt me too."

"I don't want to fight you, my friend," Aeris said.

"You have to," Dothar said, standing ready with his sword. "Or I will kill you."

Aeris drew his sword.

Dothar adjusted his stance.

"You know I will win," Aeris said. "You're the eyes, I'm the fighter. That's why they send us together."

"I can't just let you walk away," Dothar said.

"You won't," Aeris said.

Aeris jumped forward at Dothar.

Dothar was able to raise his sword to block the overhead blow that Aeris made sure Dothar had time to read. While Dothar's attention was on the swords above his head, Aeris punched his friend in the face with his free hand, knocking him to the ground. Dothar's sword fell a few feet out of his reach.

Dothar looked up at Aeris from the snow-covered earth, panic on his face.

"Make it quick," he pleaded.

Aeris stepped forward and knocked Dothar in the head with the butt of his sword, knocking his friend unconscious.

Aeris stared down at Dothar lying in the snow. It reminded him of his first kill. When he looked down at Sagewalker, lying at his feet, with the Ice King staring through him.

"Sorry my friend," Aeris said. "But this way, you didn't just let me go."

Aeris turned and left Dothar in the cold wet snow, abandoned in the middle of the clearing. He hoped he was doing the right thing.

*

Aeris didn't even know where he was heading. He didn't know of any sorcerers. Or where to find them.

He just figured he would continue on, into the forbidden territory. Areas he didn't recognize and had never been to at least held a chance of finding something. More than the familiar snowy mountaintops where the hunt was constant.

He started descending in altitude. Making his way down the mountain.

To areas he had never seen before.

The trees started to change, the snow became patchy and more shallow.

Dirt and bare ground appeared beneath the trees.

He bent down to touch the bare earth. He had never seen bare earth before. The mountains that he was so familiar with were always covered with snow. He ran his fingers through the dirt and pine needles and smelled bare earth for the first time. It smelled fresh and even familiar.

He took a moment to admire the root systems that were exposed around the bottom of the trees and the pine cones that lay on the ground around them.

Aeris stood up and looked at the road ahead of him and then back up at the snowy mountains that he was leaving behind.

He took a deep breath and continued forward towards the lower altitudes.

As he got farther down the mountain, Aeris started to feel dizzy. He shook off the lightheadedness and tried to continue his journey. Soon, he felt an ache in his head and had to sit down for a rest.

Aeris found a tree to lean against and slid down it and sat on the ground, with his back supported by the thick trunk. He drew his knees up and put his head forward. He held onto the sides of his head to try to stop the spinning feeling he was experiencing.

He thought that he would just rest for a moment, but he quickly dropped off into sleep.

*

"Hey, man," a voice said. "Are you all right?"

Aeris woke to someone shaking him by the shoulder.

"Is he ok?" another voice asked.

"I think he was just asleep," the first voice said.

Aeris felt his head clearing and tried to stand up, his legs wobbled beneath him and he staggered sideways into a person who was several heads shorter than he was. He tried to draw his sword, but was stopped by helpful hands that tried to steady him.

When his vision cleared, he saw a young woman standing in front of him wearing flimsy brown leather armor and two young men behind her. One was wearing the robe of a friar, the other was dressed colorfully, in a manner that he did not recognize.

Only one was armed, that he could see, and that was the woman. The knife at her side didn't look dangerous. Nor was it positioned on her body in an effective position for fighting.

Aeris let his eyes come into focus and laid one hand on the sword at his side, but he did not draw it. Yet.

"Nice armor," the woman said. "You must have spent a fortune on that."

Aeris looked past the three in front of him and scanned the tree line. There were no others hiding in the woods. The light was bright. The dark sky was gone, and the sky above him was a light blue and the brightness hurt his eyes. He had to squint and look away from the sky, so he brought his focus back to the party in front of him.

"Are you okay?" the woman asked again.

"Yes," Aeris said. "Who are you?"

"I'm Jennifer," she said. "I mean, I'm Priscilla Red Thorn. And these are my companions, Friar Gelfroy and Cooper."

Aeris nodded to the friar and then looked to the other man.

"Cooper?" he asked.

"Yeah," the friar answered. "He's new. Hasn't picked a persona yet."

"Stay in character," Priscilla smacked the friar with the back of her hand.

"You just hit a friar," Aeris said, truly surprised for the first time.

"See?" Priscilla said to the friar. "He gets it."

"You guys take this way too seriously," Cooper said.

"What's your name?" Priscilla ignored Cooper and focused on Aeris.

"I'm Aeris Jagger, leader of the elf rangers, and member of the Wild Hunt."

"Wow," Cooper said. "Okay, if I'm going to do this, I need a cool name like that. That's way better than what you guys say."

"Oh wow," Priscilla said. "I just noticed the ears. How did you get them to look so real?"

She reached out to touch Aeris' ear.

Aeris stepped back and half drew his sword with a metallic hiss from the blade.

"Don't touch," Aeris said.

"Okay, okay," Priscilla backed away with her hands up. "Don't be so high-strung."

"I need to find a sorcerer," Aeris said. "Do you know of one?"

"How about a sorceress?" Priscilla asked.

"Yeah, I think one of the booths has a fortune teller or something," Cooper said. "I remember seeing one when we got lunch."

"Lunch?" Aeris stared at Cooper.

"Yeah, lunch," Friar Gelfroy said. "You hungry? Cuz, I could eat another one of those turkey legs."

Aeris nodded slightly and gestured for the party to lead the way. "I would be in your debt if you would lead me to the sorceress."

"We're here to help," Priscilla grinned. "You have my word."

The three headed back down the hill and Aeris followed them closely.

Soon, the trees became sparser and Aeris was getting used to the brightness. He felt like he couldn't look up at the sky due to the brightness of the sun, but he was able to scan his surroundings.

He could hear music and people chattering in the distance, and the smell of cooked meat became stronger and stronger until it felt overwhelming to his elf senses. He could smell horses, and other odors he couldn't identify.

They came upon a small town, with rickety looking shacks and colorful tents and various booths filled with people selling wares. Jewelry, clothing, small weapons, food, drinks. Aeris drew stares from most of the people he passed. He was a full head taller than even the tallest man and he did not see another elf anywhere. In fact, he didn't see anything but humans.

"Nice ears," a man taunted as he walked past. "This isn't a Con."

Aeris glared hard at the man, who stumbled backwards in fear of Aeris' gaze, making him trip over a barrel that was set in front of a jewelry stand. The lady running the stand scolded the man for not being careful as the party moved on.

Aeris could hear the woman still berating the man as they walked away and he chuckled to himself.

He followed Cooper, the strangely dressed man, until they reached a purple tent. The front was closed up and a wood sign stood in front of the entryway. Burned into the grain were the words, *"Be Back Soon"*.

Priscilla sighed, "We missed her."

"She'll be back," Gelfroy pointed at the sign. "Why don't we feed Aeris in the meantime?"

"Feed Aeris?" Cooper mocked.

"Yes," Aeris said. "I'm hungry."

Aeris couldn't remember the last time he had eaten. He couldn't remember the last time he felt hungry.

He felt a hollow grumbling in his stomach that felt vaguely like hunger, although he could never remember feeling that way during the hunt.

Friar Gelfroy led the way to a stand that was selling whole turkey legs.

"None for me," Priscilla said when they got there.

Aeris inhaled the scent of cooking meat. He couldn't remember anything ever smelling so good during his time in the hunt. This was a scent he was sure he would remember, but it only rang as vaguely familiar. A memory that was far away and out of his reach, but still there.

Gelfroy and Cooper went forward in the small crowd and returned, each holding two turkey legs.

"I said none for me," Priscilla said.

"I didn't get you one," Friar Gelfroy said. He held a turkey leg, one in each hand, and took a bite of each in turn and smiled at Priscilla through a mouthful of meat.

"That's gross," she said.

Cooper also held a turkey leg in each hand, but one he held out to Aeris.

"Thank you," Aeris said, taking the leg from Cooper.

Aeris took a bite of the turkey leg. It was meaty and plump and dripping with juiciness. Aeris had to use a napkin that Cooper handed to him to keep the drippings from running down his arm and getting his gauntlets wet. He wrapped the bone with the strange paper and continued to eat.

"Man, he was hungry," Cooper said as he watched Aeris devour the leg.

"Yeah," Gelfroy said, holding two now empty legs himself. "I've never seen anyone eat that fast."

Priscilla looked at Gelfroy, "Get a mirror."

"Ha-ha," Gelfroy said. "Funny."

Cooper looked around and found a trash can. "Over here."

He dropped the bone and his wet napkins into the can and Gelfroy did the same. Aeris just followed their lead and dropped his bone in the trash.

He looked into the can and saw all manner of things he couldn't identify. Strange see-through bottles and other various items.

Priscilla looked over curiously to see what was so interesting in the can. She followed his gaze and then asked, "Oh, do you need some water? I'm thirsty too."

She turned and headed into the crowd. The three men immediately followed her. They hung back while she disappeared into a line and returned a few minutes later with four clear bottles, with water dripping down the sides.

She handed one to each of them and shook the wet from her free hand before unscrewing the blue top from the bottle.

When Aeris took the bottle from her, he was surprised by two things. He wasn't expecting the bottle to be as cold as it was, especially not during the warm afternoon. Nor was he expecting how flimsy the bottle felt in his hand.

He unscrewed the blue lid and took a swig from the bottle. It was clear, fresh and cold, but with a strange, unfamiliar tinge of flavor. He didn't like it, but drank anyway. Thirst was more important than taste.

"Why don't we see if the fortune teller is back yet?" Cooper suggested.

"Good idea," Priscilla said. "People don't usually leave their booths unattended for long here."

They made their way back to the purple tent. This time, the sign was gone and the tent flap was pulled back, to indicate that she was open and not with a client.

There was a small table and two rickety looking chairs in front of the tent. The table was covered with a bright red tablecloth with Runic patterns printed on it.

As they made their way forward, a woman came out of the tent. She was dressed in a puffy blouse and a skirt that displayed all manner of purples and blues in shades that Aeris couldn't ever remember seeing.

The endless nights hunting muted colors and in the eternal winter of the mountains, there were only shades of snow and shadow. So the colors, on the woman, as well as around the little village, seemed stunningly vibrant to Aeris.

She wore lots of jewelry, earrings, chains around her neck, many bracelets were wrapped around her wrists, and she wore a ring on every finger.

Around her waist was a belt made of dangling coins that jingled noisily when she walked.

She had a black scarf wrapped around her head and the long ends of it trailed down over one shoulder along with a mass of her long wavy brown hair.

When she saw them approach, she looked pleased, but when she saw Aeris, a momentary look of shock displayed on her face and then vanished just as quickly.

"Welcome," she said in an accented voice. "Would any of you like your fortune told?"

She smiled sweetly and looked at Priscilla, "How about you?" She took Priscilla's hand and opened her palm to look at it. "I can read your love line and tell you what a life you have in store!"

"Actually, my friend Aeris is the one who wanted to see you," Priscilla gently pulled her hand away and gestured back to Aeris.

He stepped forward to stand next to Priscilla.

Aeris stared down at the woman. He could see her more clearly now. She wore heavy makeup and most of her jewelry was leather and crystal or other stones. All of it looked handmade.

She stared Aeris up and down and then gestured inside her tent.

"We must go in," she said. "To talk in private."

She led the way into her tent. Aeris followed.

Inside, there was a purple velvet chair that looked like a small throne and a deep red Victorian era loveseat facing the chair. A small, but sturdy, ornately carved wooden table stood between them. There were colorful rugs scattered all over the floor and lots of Moroccan style pillows everywhere.

A cabinet overflowing with herbs, glass jars and bottles, and crystals was in the corner near the back and a small table near the door stood holding a crystal ball and a deck of old-fashioned looking Tarot cards.

"My name is Sabina," she said dropping her thick accent.

She watched as Priscilla, Cooper, and Gelfroy followed them into the tent.

"Do you want them here too?" she asked Aeris.

Aeris glanced back at the three he had been traveling with. "They have helped me get this far; they can stay."

Sabina eyed them and gestured for them to take a seat among the flood of pillows on the floor. They silently obeyed, and sat side by side, near the loveseat and chair.

"Have a seat," she gestured to the loveseat.

Aeris removed his bow and quiver and laid them on the floor next to the couch, in front of his three friends. They watched wide-eyed as he moved swiftly, like the weapons weren't as cumbersome as they looked.

He flipped his cape aside and adjusted his swords so that he could sit on the front edge of the couch.

Sabina sat down across from him, smoothing her full skirt under herself and letting the fabric flow down the sides of the chair to the floor in a cascade of color.

"Let me see your hands," Sabina put her heavily jeweled hands, palms up, on the table.

Aeris glanced at his friends for a moment. They nodded in encouragement.

Aeris then proceeded to remove his gauntlets and gloves. The process took a few moments as he undid clasps and buckles. He placed the hand and wrist wear on the couch behind himself as he removed each item.

When he was finished, he placed his hands in Sabina's patiently waiting hands that had remained outstretched on the table during the entire process.

She spent several minutes in silence, examining his palms and frowning.

"It's just as I thought," she said, still frowning.

"What is?" Gelfroy asked.

Sabina frowned at Gelfroy, who was shushed by Priscilla at the same moment.

Sabina looked back to Aeris. "I could sense the moment I saw you that you were not from here."

"You got that vibe too, did ya?" Cooper smirked.

Priscilla shushed Cooper too.

Sabina ignored Cooper and continued. "You are looking for your memories, no?"

"How did you?" Aeris was taken aback. "I haven't told you why I'm here."

Sabina sat back in her chair. "Some people come for their fortunes told. They want a show and to be told that they are going to be rich and famous. Any of the fortune tellers here can play the part, say the right words, and the client leaves happy."

She glanced over to the three on the floor and then back to Aeris.

"Then there are those like you," she wagged a finger at Aeris. "You were destined to come here, to me. To someone who is not merely an actor playing a part. To someone who can tell you what it is that you truly need to know."

"You're telling me that destiny made you the first booth at the edge of the faire?" Cooper asked.

Sabina glared at Cooper. Priscilla shushed him again.

Sabina looked back to Aeris. "Close your eyes and think back as far as you can remember."

Aeris complied and he and Sabina sat quietly as she held his hands with her eyes shut too.

After a few minutes, she opened her eyes and looked at Aeris closely. She let go of his hands and sighed.

"Your memories are fae-touched," she said.

"What does that mean?" Priscilla asked, leaning forward with interest.

"It means that his mind has been altered in some way," Sabina said.

"So, his memories are fake?" Gelfroy asked.

"No," Sabina said. "His memories are real, but there are others. Other memories. From before. They have been stolen."

"Stolen?" Aeris frowned at Sabina. "What do you mean by stolen?"

Sabina took a deep breath. "I don't know. They are just not there. There are definite signs of magic. Fae magic. Certain types of fae can steal memories."

"Can he get them back?" Priscilla asked.

"I don't know," Sabina said. "But your best chance is by finding the fae who stole them in the first place."

"Then what do I do?" Aeris asked.

Sabina shrugged, "It depends on the fae."

"What does he have to do?" Priscilla asked. "Just ask for them back?"

"Or kill 'em?" Cooper asked.

Sabina looked at them, and then back to Aeris. "I don't know. That you will have to figure out when you find the fae that stole them."

Aeris sat for a moment, "I think I know who stole them."

"That's a good start," Priscilla said. "Where do we look?"

Aeris glanced at Priscilla and back to Sabina.

"Do you know the type of fae?" Sabina asked. "Knowing could help a lot."

"He's the Ice King," Aeris said.

Sabina sat back in her chair, with a look of sheer horror on her face.

"The Ice King?" Cooper said. "He should be easy to fight. Just bring a flame-thrower with you."

Aeris looked at Cooper, "Where can I find a flame-thrower?"

Sabina shook her head, "It won't help. The Ice King doesn't fear fire."

"That just sounds wrong," Gelfroy said. "Ice should be afraid of fire."

"He is not made of ice," Sabina said. "It not that simple."

"Then what is he made of?" Cooper asked.

"You saw the Wild Hunt, didn't you?" Sabina asked.

"I am a member of the Wild Hunt," Aeris said.

"You're what?" Sabina stood up, almost knocking her heavy chair over. "You're a member of the Wild Hunt? How are you here?"

"I came down the mountain," Aeris said.

"You must leave," Sabina said, pointing to the doorway. "You must leave here now."

"Why? What's wrong?" Priscilla said.

"You must leave him," Sabina said to Priscilla. "You must let him go back, and never lay eyes on him again."

"Why?" Cooper was standing now too. "What is the Wild Hunt?"

"Anyone who lays eyes on the Wild Hunt must join or die," Sabina said. "He is part of the Hunt. They will come for him. Leave this place. Now. Or you will cost everyone here their lives."

"Like all of us?" Gelfroy asked, now standing too.

"Everyone," Sabina said, almost panicking now. "Anyone who has seen him today. Anyone who sees the hunting party that is looking for him. Hundreds of people could die."

"We need to go," Priscilla said, pulling Aeris by the arm. "We need to go now."

Aeris bent over and picked up his bow and quiver and slung them over his shoulder. He grabbed his gloves and gauntlets and started pulling them back on his hands.

He looked at Sabina, "I'm sorry."

"Leave," Sabina demanded. Tears were welling up in her eyes. "Leave now!"

"Thank you for the information," Priscilla said to Sabina. "What do we owe you?"

"Nothing," Sabina cried. "Get out now. All of you. And if you're smart, you will get as far away from him as possible."

Priscilla ushered the three men out of the tent and back into the glaringly bright sunlight.

"Now what?" Gelfroy asked.

"We take him back to where we found him and send him back up the mountain," Cooper said. "That's what."

"We can't just abandon him," Priscilla said. "I gave him my word that we would help him."

"We have," Gelfroy said. "We helped him figure out what he has to do. Now he's on his own."

"We said we'd help him," Priscilla said.

"This isn't a game," Cooper said. "Didn't you hear what that woman said?"

"Oh, you believe in fortune tellers now?" Priscilla mocked. "You didn't seem to when we got there."

"Stop it," Aeris said. "I will go back up the mountain. You will all be safe."

"All right," Priscilla started walking towards the woods. "Let's go."

"You don't need to go," Aeris said.

"We can at least escort you to where we found you," Priscilla said. "To make sure you find the right way back."

Aeris nodded and started his way to the woods.

"Awh, Pris," Gelfroy kicked at the dirt. "You and your stinkin' loyalty."

"We can at least do that," Cooper agreed. "Take him back to where we found him."

"So, you actually believe all of this?" Priscilla asked.

Cooper shrugged, "What else is there to do?"

Gelfroy gestured back to the colorful tents and booths that they were leaving behind, "Uhm, there's a whole faire going on back there. Didn't you see it?"

Cooper looked back at Gelfroy and smiled, "This is more fun."

The party headed back up the base of the mountain. It was getting later and the sun was drooping lower in the sky. After they had been walking for a while, the terrain started looking unfamiliar.

"Are you sure this was the way we went?" Gelfroy asked.

Priscilla stopped and looked around. "I thought it was."

"I don't think so," Cooper said. "None of this looks familiar."

"How can you even tell?" Gelfroy whined. "It all looks the same. Pine trees everywhere."

Aeris surveyed the terrain. "It doesn't matter. I just need to go up."

"We said we would take you back to where we found you," Priscilla said.

Aeris turned and looked at the two young men who were sweating and breathing hard behind him.

"Go back," Aeris said. "You've more than kept your promise. We passed where you found me already. I just need to continue up."

"We passed it already?" Gelfroy said. "Why didn't you say something?"

"He's lying," Cooper said. "We've gone too far east. We may have passed it in altitude, but we never actually got there."

"Go back," Aeris said again. "Enjoy your faire. You've kept your promise."

Priscilla looked back down the mountain and then back at Aeris. "I'm going to keep going with you."

"Aww, Pris," Gelfroy said. "Don't. Let's just go back."

Cooper stood and looked at Priscilla, "I'm not sure that's a good idea."

"I don't care," she said. "I don't think he should be wandering around up here alone."

"But you're going to come back all alone," Cooper said. "In the dark?"

"I'll be fine," she said. "I've got more outdoor and hiking experience than both of you put together."

"No," Aeris said. "You need to go back with them."

"What?" Priscilla turned to Aeris. "I gave you my word. I have to help you."

"You have," Aeris stepped towards Priscilla and took her hands. "You have more than kept your promise. I need you to go back now. If you accidentally see the Hunt, or any other party members, it will mean your death. I don't want that on my conscience."

Cooper came up behind Priscilla and put his hand on her shoulder. "Pris, it's time to go home."

Priscilla sighed. "Take care of yourself, Aeris."

"You too," Aeris said. He squeezed her hands and then dropped them. "Thank you for your help. All of you."

He nodded to Cooper and Gelfroy.

"Be safe," Cooper said.

"Yeah, take care," Gelfroy said.

Aeris looked at Priscilla one last time and saw that her eyes were filled with tears. He looked away quickly and started up the mountain again.

"Come on, Pris," Gelfroy said. "Let's go home."

Cooper gently turned Priscilla towards the base of the mountain again, "We need to let him go. Let's go home."

The three started their way back down the mountain towards the faire.

*

Aeris continued his way back up the mountain. The patchy snow became thicker and denser as he went up in altitude, and soon he was back in the familiar carpet of white. The trees were once again iced with snow, so that it seemed that all the color had been erased from the world, leaving the blinding whiteness to burn his eyes.

The sun was fading away, leaving long shadows across the terrain. Aeris continued on up the mountain.

He wondered when exactly he would cross from the world below to the world where only the Hunt existed. He couldn't remember feeling any different anywhere on the way down. Just the altitude change.

He did enjoy listening to the silence of the snow once again. The clamor and noise of the faire had been too much for his elven ears and had made him anxious. One of the many reasons he had become a scout for the Hunt. He enjoyed the silence.

Aeris listened to the crunching of his boots in the snow. It should have been the only sound, but there was another. A lighter crunching. The steps of another. Someone, or something lighter than he was, taking heavy tired steps behind him.

He turned to see Priscilla, breathing heavily, coming up behind him.

It didn't look like her clothing would keep her warm enough in the dark chill of night that was looming.

"I told you to go back," Aeris called out to her.

"I did," she huffed. "Then I ditched the boys and came back."

"You're going to freeze to death," he said.

She made it up to where he was standing and stood panting to catch her breath.

"I'm fine," she said. "I just need to breathe for a minute."

"You need to go back down the mountain to your friends," he commanded. "You can't go with me. If you do, you will either die or never return."

"I don't believe you," she said. "I need to make sure you're okay. I promised I would help you."

Aeris sighed and looked at the ground. "I can't take you any further," he said. "So, I will take you back."

"No," Priscilla said. "I will just follow you again."

"Look at you," Aeris said. "You're not dressed for the snow, and you can't catch your breath. You're getting altitude sickness. Soon, you're going to get dizzy and get a headache."

"Already have the headache," she said.

Aeris shut his eyes for a moment to calm himself.

"I'm taking you back," he said again.

"You should know better," a voice said behind him from somewhere in the trees.

Aeris turned quickly and blocked Priscilla with his body.

"Dothar?" Aeris scanned the tree line until he could see signs of his scouting partner. "Is that you?"

"You left me to die," Dothar said. "You know that, right?"

Dothar stepped out from behind a tree so that Aeris could see him clearly. He had his sword drawn, but it was held down by his side.

"You left, and left me to face the consequences of the Hunt," Dothar said.

"I left you unconscious," Aeris said. "There's no way they could hold you responsible for my leaving."

"Yet they did," Dothar said.

"What?" Aeris was surprised.

"They know we were friends," Dothar said. "They held me responsible."

"Oh, Dothar," Aeris said. "I'm sorry."

"If you were ever truly my friend," Dothar said. "You know what you need to do."

Aeris nodded and stared at the ground.

"What?" Priscilla asked. "What do you have to do?"

"Is that a human with you?" Dothar asked.

"Yes," Aeris said. "But she has nothing to do with this. She must go back."

"It's too late," Dothar said. "You know the rules."

"It's not too late," Aeris objected.

"I'm part of the Hunt," Dothar said. "She has seen me and heard my words."

Priscilla came out from behind Aeris, "What does that mean?"

Dothar just smiled.

"It means you can never return," Aeris said.

"It also means our freedom," Dothar smiled.

"No," Aeris stepped in front of Priscilla again. "You will not use her for a surety."

"No, I won't," Dothar said. "You will."

"Never," Aeris said.

"Oh, I think you will," Dothar said, still smiling. "I will use you as my surety. You will use her. Then we can go back to things the way they used to be. Like this never happened. And we will have something to hunt."

"I said no," Aeris said.

Aeris drew his sword. Priscilla instinctively stepped back, away from him.

"I am taking this human back to where she came from," Aeris said. "If you try to stop me, I will kill you, my old friend."

"It's too late for that," Dothar said loudly. "I will use you as my surety. What you do is up to you."

From out of the trees, members of the Hunt suddenly made their appearance.

The hellhounds showed themselves first. The hairless dog-like creatures, with their muscular frames came growling and snarling forward.

Other creatures emerged, elves, creatures of the undead, fae of all kinds. They were all wearing armor and hunting gear and had their weapons drawn. Their menacing faces stared down at Aeris and Priscilla.

Aeris watched as the circle enclosed around them. There was no escape.

He looked down at Priscilla. Her eyes were wide with terror as she took in all of the creatures that were surrounding them. Her hand was on the weapon at her side, but he could tell she was too scared to draw it. There were too many creatures. She knew there was no escape.

Aeris drew in a deep breath.

He knew what he had to do.

Aeris looked at Dothar, "I will follow the rules of the Hunt."

Dothar lowered his sword and nodded once at Aeris. "I thought you might."

"What?" Priscilla asked. "What?"

He looked down at Priscilla again. Panic was all over her face.

"Don't worry," Aeris said. "It will be over quickly."

"Aeris, you can't-" she said.

"Be quiet," he commanded. "Don't say a word."

Priscilla had tears running down her face. She was gasping for air, trying to control her breathing, but she remained quiet.

"I have found Aeris Jagger, I present him as my surety," Dothar said loudly to the members of the Hunt.

Cheers came up from the crowd. They waved their weapons in the air and the hellhounds howled a spine shaking howl along with them.

Priscilla stood slightly behind Aeris, shaking violently and still trying to catch her breath.

The hunting party made room for a man - a creature - that looked like something undead. He was extremely tall, dwarfing the centaurs as he passed them. His wrinkled and rotting skin was tinted a light blue in the moonlight and he was wearing animal furs over his leather and iron clad armor. He had an ax with a long handle and he carried it like he was ready to swing it at any time. On his head he wore a crown that looked like it was made of bones and ice.

His cold eyes settled on Priscilla and she felt like they were boring a hole through her. She started shivering harder, and she felt like her bones were being changed into ice. She felt like she would never be warm again.

She let out a sharp cry and Aeris reached out with his sword and put it to the Ice King's throat.

"Leave her alone," Aeris growled.

The Ice King changed his focus and stared at Aeris.

As a member of the Hunt, the icy stare did not have the same effect on Aeris. He just wanted to draw the Ice King's attention from Priscilla.

"You dare to draw your weapon at me?" the Ice King said.

"It's in the rules," Aeris said.

"To which rule would you be referring?" the Ice King asked.

"The rule that says I can challenge you," Aeris said.

The Ice King laughed. It echoed through the trees and shook the snow from the branches. The hunting party joined in the Ice King's laughter.

"No one has ever defeated me," the Ice King mocked. "You would be better off offering the human as your surety."

"Never," Aeris said.

"Really?" the Ice King said, slowly walking a circle around Aeris.

Aeris followed the Ice King with his blade, pivoting with the creature as it moved around him and Priscilla.

"She would be such a lovely quarry," the Ice King said. "And you-"

The Ice King looked at Aeris, "You have been one of our best scouts. I would hate to lose you, Aeris."

"You will lose me tonight," Aeris said. "Because one of us is going to die."

"No one has ever defeated me," the Ice King reminded him. "When I win, she will be our quarry anyway. So why don't you put down your sword and just present your surety. There is no reason for you to die here tonight alongside of her."

Aeris refused to lower his sword, "I, Aeris Jagger, challenge you, Ice King, to a battle to the death," Aeris said loudly. "For your crown. And for her."

Aeris indicated Priscilla with a slight nod of his head.

The Ice King laughed again. This time, the creatures didn't laugh with him.

Instead, they cheered and closed the circle around the two Huntsmen and Priscilla.

"Even if you win," the Ice King said. "You cannot set her free."

"When I win," Aeris said. "She will be no one's surety, and she will join us in the Hunt."

"A human woman?" the Ice King glanced at Priscilla. "You are dreaming, elf boy. You will lose, and she will be our pretty-pretty prey."

The two Huntsmen started to circle one another. The Ice King readied his ax and Aeris put his other hand on the hilt of his sword.

Priscilla tried to circle away from Aeris and the Ice King without getting too close to any of the creatures in the circle. She was still freezing cold and shivering harder than she ever had in her life.

As Aeris circled the Ice King in front of her, he unhooked his cape and swung it over to her in one swift movement, never once taking his eyes off of the Ice King.

Priscilla scurried forward and grabbed the cape from the snow and pulled the wool garment tightly around herself. It gave her slight relief from the frigid cold that she could still feel down to her bones.

The Ice King lunged forward, swinging his ax to make the first blow. Aeris deftly blocked the ax with his sword.

Priscilla cringed when the two metal weapons clanged against one another for the first time. It was much louder than she thought it would be.

The roar of the creatures surrounding the fight soon was loud enough to muffle the blows of the metal weapons.

The Ice King and Aeris continued to attempt to land blows on each other as Priscilla tried to stay out of the way.

It was obvious that the Ice King was much stronger than Aeris. His blows were taking an obvious toll on the stamina of the elf.

Aeris swung his blade towards the Ice King and missed completely, but this made an opening that the Ice King took advantage of. He swung his ax and it struck Aeris in the side, sliding into flesh right above the armor, into Aeris' armpit.

"No!" Priscilla screamed.

Aeris staggered backwards and fell to his knees in pain. He watched his own blood stream down onto the white snow.

The Ice King stepped forward and was about to land another blow on Aeris, but the elf swung his sword and dug it deeply into the Ice King's leg. The Ice King fell himself, but still landed a sidelong blow to Aeris' shoulder, near his neck.

Aeris slumped forward, with even more blood gushing from the new wound.

The Ice King, on one knee next to Aeris, drew his ax up again.

Priscilla rushed forward and pulled her sword from her scabbard. She took the small blade and lifted it high in the air. She stopped behind the Ice King and drove the sword down into the back of his neck, piercing the blue flesh through to the front of his throat.

The Ice King dropped his ax to the snow next to him, never landing the last blow to Aeris. He slumped forward, dead in the snow. His crown of bones and ice fell off and rolled across the snow and stopped at Dothar's feet.

Priscilla rushed over to Aeris' side and grabbed him by the shoulders, to set him up straight.

"You can't die, Aeris," she said, tears streaming down her face.

Aeris looked up at her and put his hand to her face. "I'm sorry," he said. "For everything."

Dothar approached, holding the Ice King's crown by his side, and he knelt down at Aeris' side.

"My friend," he said. He put his hand on Aeris' shoulder.

"Watch out for her," Aeris pleaded.

"I will be the servant and protector of the Queen," Dothar said.

"What?" Priscilla looked at Dothar.

He took the Ice King's crown with both hands, and while kneeling in front of Priscilla, he placed the crown on her head.

The roar from the crowd of creatures was deafening. Priscilla looked from Dothar and back to Aeris. She was still holding onto him when he slumped forward and breathed his last breath.

She knelt in the snow, next to Dothar as they both said goodbye to their friend.

The creatures started chanting, "Ice Queen! Ice Queen!"

Dothar put his hand out to Priscilla. She took it and he helped her stand up.

As she rose to her feet, she felt her bones turn to ice. The cold emanated out from her bones and, instead of her freezing to death, she felt comfortable.

She looked at her arms and ice started forming on her skin. Icicles sprouted from her pores and froze into place. Her hair started to cover with frost and her clothing, including Aeris' cape, turned white as the snow.

She took a deep breath and breathed the cold air clearly into her lungs and exhaled the condensation visibly into the air.

When she turned to face the creatures that crowded around her, she faced them as their Queen.

Priscilla is Queen of The Wild Hunt. But with the Ice King's followers against her, how long can she maintain her reign? Here is the third and final story of The Wild Hunt trilogy.

Priscilla Reigns

Priscilla stood atop a high snowbank, and leaned on her long-handled ax. Her dark woolen cape flowed down to the snow at her feet, but she had no need to keep warm.

The ice that formed on her skin never felt cold to her, nor did the chill of the winter air. The crown that she wore on her head was made of bone and ice, and even more importantly, magic.

The ice magic froze her bones as soon as the crown had been placed on her head by Dothar, just before her friend Aeris died. Just after she killed the Ice King. She emanated cold herself and could cause lesser beings to freeze to death with a stare.

She could still remember the battle, but just barely. Aeris and the Ice King battling for the crown that she now wore. They were also battling for her. The thoughts slipped from her grasp, but she knew that the winner of that battle would get the crown and her as well. The Ice King wanted to hunt her. Aeris wanted to free her. Or at least free her from being hunted.

What Aeris had really wanted was to send her home.

Priscilla looked out across the snowy landscape of the mountain and tried to remember home. She tried to remember anything before the Ice Crown was placed on her head. Anything before the moment that she had driven her knife into the back of the Ice King's neck.

She was on treacherous ground. The Ice King had a loyal following. When she had killed him, some of his faithful hunters didn't think how she killed him was within the rules. There were some in the Wild Hunt that didn't think that she should be Queen.

She had been challenged several times already. Challenged by some of the ones who felt she shouldn't be their leader.

Dothar had promised Aeris that he would keep the Queen safe. He swore to be her servant and protector. When the Queen was challenged, Dothar stepped in to be her champion and fought in her place.

Dothar remained undefeated.

As a result, Priscilla remained Queen.

The members of the Hunt ran across a clearing below, in pursuit of whatever it was that they were chasing that night. Night elves, the undead, centaurs, and other magical creatures were led by the hairless but muscular hellhounds who always seemed to be on the scent of something.

Priscilla tried to remember if they had ever caught anything. Or if the Wild Hunt was a futile endeavor. She wondered if they were all doomed to hunt forever, but never to catch their prey.

Dothar came up behind her and watched the Hunt race by down below. They stood quietly as the cacophony of the hunters yelled and cheered as they went.

"Do you think there is even anything out there?" Priscilla asked. "Or do you think they scare everything away with their noise?"

"Aeris didn't think there was anything there," Dothar said quietly.

Priscilla turned and looked at her protector.

"He said that?" she asked.

Dothar nodded, "Just before he found you."

"Tell me again what happened that night," Priscilla said.

Dothar shrugged, "Aeris was tired of chasing nothing. So, he went in search of his memories. He came back with you. That's all I know."

"There has to be more to it than that," Priscilla said.

"I'm sure there is," Dothar said. "But I'm not privy to it."

Priscilla stared down at the now quiet clearing. She could still hear the hunters in the distance, but she was lost in thought.

"I want to know where he went," she said. "I want to know where I came from."

Dothar sighed. "You can't. Nobody leaves the Hunt, or they become the hunted. That's the only time I can ever remember catching anything. When someone tries to leave."

"So, you hunt nothing until the time comes to hunt each other?" she stared at Dothar.

He paused before saying, "Apparently."

"Haven't you ever wondered what is down there?" Priscilla stared down the mountain. "What there is outside of the Hunt?"

"Not until Aeris started questioning it," Dothar replied. "Since then, I have thought of nothing else."

"Come with me," she said.

"What?" Dothar stared at the Ice Queen with wide eyes. "We can't."

"Why not?" she asked.

"They will hunt us," he replied.

"They never go down the mountain," she continued to stare down the mountain, into the darkness that engulfed the world below them. "And they challenge us constantly anyway. What difference will it make?"

"It's against the rules," Dothar said.

"Whose rules?" she asked. "I am the Queen; don't I get a say in the rules?"

"I-I don't-" Dothar started, but he stopped and scrunched his brow looking deep in thought. "I don't know who made the rules. Or where they came from."

"Then we will go," she said. "I am making a rule that you and I can go scout down below."

Dothar looked back at where the Hunt had raced through the clearing at the base of the snow bank. "I don't want to become the hunted."

"I am going to scout below," she said, as she started to move. "And you will come with me because you made a promise to Aeris to be my protector."

Dothar stepped in front of her, "As your protector, I advise you to not do this."

"And as your Queen I command you to move out of my way and come with me," she said. She placed her hand on his chest and moved him aside and started her way down the mountain.

"This is twice Aeris has put my life in danger because of this stupid mountain," Dothar muttered as he followed his Queen.

*

After travelling for what seemed like hours, Dothar and the Queen could see light below.

"What is that?" she asked.

"I think it's daylight," Dothar said.

"I feel like I should remember the sun," Priscilla said. "But I can't."

"I know," Dothar said. "It's like it's right there, but then as soon as you lock onto the thought, it disappears like the wind."

Priscilla nodded.

"I think I need to rest," Priscilla said. She was breathing hard and found a tree to sit under.

The snow was getting more and more sparse, showing dirt and pine needles and even the roots of the trees.

Priscilla concentrated on her breathing and felt like lead was filling her lungs. The air felt heavy and the scent of the pine trees was thick in the air.

Dothar stood next to her and took in their surroundings.

"I think we've scouted enough," he said.

Priscilla could hear the fact that Dothar was winded in his voice. There was a slight gasping as he spoke.

"Rest with me," she said. "Sit."

Dothar reluctantly came down to one knee, still looking around at their surroundings.

"The air is too thick for us here," Dothar said. "We need to go back."

"Not yet," the Queen said. "We have scouted nothing yet. We've barely made it down the mountain."

Before Dothar could object, Priscilla leaned on her ax and stood up. Her head swam slightly, making her feel nauseous. She rested, leaning on her ax handle and breathing deeply, until she felt stable again.

"Are you ready?" she asked Dothar.

He sighed and got to his feet, "Yes, my Queen."

The sun was just peeking its way over the horizon. The early morning light illuminated their way.

They found a foot path as they neared the bottom of the mountain. Priscilla followed it, hoping it could lead her to the answers that she sought.

Instead, it led her to what looked like a small abandoned village. There were a few buildings here and there and many small structures that looked as if they could be merchants' booths. The wood was old, but still sturdy, and everything looked ramshackle and weather worn. The small buildings were locked up and the small tents were empty.

Everything was centered around a large area with an empty clearing. A small stage was off to one side, and at the far end of the little village was a jousting arena. Dothar lingered at it, staring at the field where the riders would race towards one another and compete in the tournament.

"Do this bring back memories?" Priscilla asked.

"I don't know," Dothar said.

She could tell he was lost in thought. Caught up in the almost-memories that she knew he must be experiencing. Just like she was.

She was having them too. Those moments where she could almost remember. Something she saw or smelled triggered a memory, but it flitted away like a butterfly before she could lock onto it and live the thought. It was a constant battle with deja vu and the evaporation of the memory before it could start.

As Priscilla walked among the small wooden buildings, she lingered in front of a few here and there. One smelled faintly of cooked meat, reminding her of something, or someone she may have known.

She stopped at an empty space. There was nothing there but slightly trampled ground, and several holes that could have held tent poles. She stared at the ground for a moment, wondering what kind of tent must have been staked down there. It was at the edge of everything, a place that would easily have been walked past as one entered the area. But somehow, Priscilla thought it was familiar. Important. Much more important than any other building still standing. The tent was missing, just like the memory of it.

She felt like there was something she should remember about that particular place. But nothing came to her. Nothing but the vague sense that she couldn't quite grasp onto what was forgotten.

"There's nothing here," Dothar said. "This place is totally abandoned."

"There must be something," she said. "I can feel it."

Dothar glanced back at the jousting arena. "We won't remember anything. Just thoughts that turn to mist."

"Mist can become solid," Priscilla said. "We just need the right circumstances."

"And what circumstances might those be?" Dothar asked.

"We'll have to wait and find out," she said.

They continued walking through the shabby little town, peering into empty stalls and small buildings. They finally rounded back to where they started and stood looking helplessly at the abandoned area.

"It's all deserted," Dothar said. "There's nothing to find here."

"There's something here," Priscilla said. "I can feel it."

Dothar glanced over at the jousting arena and then back to his Queen, "There's nothing."

Priscilla sighed and glanced back towards the footpath that would take them back the way they had come. Back up the mountain.

"We've been gone long enough," Dothar said. "We should go back."

Priscilla was about to relent when she heard a voice calling out behind her.

"Pris?" the voice said. "Priscilla, is that you?"

Priscilla turned and saw two young men heading towards her. One was dressed in clothing that was unfamiliar to her. Blue pants, and lightweight tunic with writing on the front of his shirt. The other was dressed like a friar.

"Do I know you?" she asked as they approached.

"Jen?" the friar said. "Is that really you?"

"I am Priscilla, the Ice Queen of the Wild Hunt," she said, standing tall and brandishing her hunting ax. "Do I know you?"

The two men stood before her and just stared at her.

"Is that real ice?" the strangely dressed one asked.

"Pris, what happened to you?" the friar asked.

"You know me?" Priscilla relaxed slightly and lowered her ax.

"We've known you for years," the friar said. "You've been missing for a week."

"A week?" she repeated. "I've been Queen for months."

Priscilla looked at Dothar.

Dothar shrugged, "It feels like years."

"Who are you?" Priscilla asked the men.

"I'm Jase Gelfroy," the friar said. "And this is Jonathan Cooper."

"We've been friends for years," Cooper said. "And your real name is Jennifer."

"But you went by Priscilla Red Thorn when we did cosplay or went to faires," Gelfroy said.

"How did you know my name was Red Thorn?" Priscilla said. "I didn't tell you."

"Yes, you did," Gelfroy said. "We were both with you when you made it up."

Priscilla thought for a moment.

"Can you tell me what happened before I disappeared?" she asked.

"We found some elf dude named Aeris up in the woods," Cooper started.

"Yeah, his armor was so cool," Gelfroy said.

"Wait," Dothar stopped him. "You knew Aeris?"

"Yeah, he was the one who started this whole thing," Cooper said. "Searching for his memories. Freaking out the fortune teller. He went back up the mountain and Priscilla followed him. We haven't seen her since."

"We've been coming back to the faire every day to look for her in the hills," Friar Gelfroy said. "Even during the week, when it's shut down."

"It shuts down?" Dothar asked.

"It's only on the weekends here," Cooper explained. "People should be coming back to set up for the day any second. We sneak in early so we don't have to pay."

"What is this place?" Priscilla asked.

"It's a faire," Cooper started.

"No," Priscilla stopped him. "What was here?"

She pointed at the ground where they were standing. Where the tent holes in the ground were the only thing left amongst the smashed down weeds and dirt.

"The fortune teller," Gelfroy said. "The one Aeris talked to. He scared her."

"Yeah," Cooper said. "She packed up that day and didn't come back."

"She was gone before we got back from leading Aeris back up the mountain," Gelfroy said.

"So, he never got the answers he was looking for?" Priscilla asked.

"She said that he had to kill the creature that stole his memories," Cooper said. "The Ice King, I think."

"Then when she found out that he was a member of the Wild Hunt, she made him leave. And she left pretty fast too," Gelfroy said.

"Yeah, she said something about anyone who sees the Wild Hunt has to join or die," Cooper said.

There was silence for a moment as they stared at one another.

"Oh no, Pris," Gelfroy said. "It's true, isn't it?"

"What is?" Cooper asked.

"Look at her," Gelfroy gestured to Priscilla. "She went up the mountain with Aeris, she must have seen the Wild Hunt. She had to join."

Cooper's face changed from confusion to anger. "It's because of Aeris, isn't it? I'll kill him if he ever comes down that mountain again."

"He's dead," Dothar said flatly.

"What?" Gelfroy gasped. "What do you mean he's dead?"

"They wanted to hunt me," Priscilla said. "He battled the Ice King to save my life."

"And you wound up having to join instead?" Gelfroy asked.

"But if he's dead, and you're here, then who killed him?" Cooper asked.

"The Ice King," Dothar said. "During the battle."

"Wait, I'm confused," Cooper said. "If the Ice King killed him in battle, how did you survive?"

Priscilla and Dothar looked at one another and then back at the two men.

"I killed the Ice King," Priscilla said.

They both gasped.

Gelfroy looked horrified, "You killed someone?"

"Something," Dothar corrected.

Cooper started to laugh joyously, "You killed the Ice King? That's so awesome!"

Gelfroy looked at Cooper in horror, "This isn't a game. Look at her!"

Cooper held his hand up in the air towards Priscilla.

She just stared at his palm.

"It's for a high five," Cooper said. "You slap my hand with yours. Don't leave me hanging."

Priscilla took a step forward and slapped Coopers palm awkwardly with her own.

Cooper reeled back in pain and stared at his hand.

"Your hand is like an ice block," Cooper looked at his palm. He tucked his hand under his arm to try to warm it up.

Gelfroy looked concerned. "Let me see your hand."

He reached out to Priscilla. She extended her hand and he touched her skin gently.

"You're frozen," Gelfroy examined her hand. "You emanate cold."

"She took on the Ice King's powers when he died," Dothar explained. "She now wears his crown."

"Wait," Gelfroy said. "You mean, she's an ice queen?"

"She is the Ice Queen, Leader of the Wild Hunt," Dothar said.

"So, like, you're in charge?" Cooper asked, still trying to warm up his hand.

"She is the leader of the Wild Hunt," Dothar said. "She is our Queen."

"And who are you?" Cooper asked.

"I am Dothar, the Queen's Champion and Protector," Dothar said.

"How do I know you two?" Priscilla asked.

"You lost your memories just like Aeris did?" Gelfroy asked. "But the Ice King is dead. So, he wasn't the one to steal them."

"We've been friends forever," Cooper said. "There were four of us. In our gaming group."

"Yeah, Eli disappeared awhile back," Gelfroy said. "He was my roommate. And the three of us. We were inseparable."

"We came to the faire to try to cheer ourselves up," Cooper said. "Because the police had decided to stop looking for Eli."

"And then you disappeared with Aeris," Gelfroy said. "It was like you wouldn't leave him."

"Which is weird," Cooper said. "Because you never showed that much interest in anyone but Eli before."

There was movement behind them, in the faire grounds.

"We'd better get you two out of here," Gelfroy said. "We don't want anyone else to see you."

"Yeah," Cooper agreed. "It's bad enough we've seen two more members of the Wild Hunt. We don't want to endanger anyone else."

Gelfroy and Cooper ushered Priscilla and Dothar back towards the path leading to the forest at the base of the mountain.

When they were far out of sight of the faire grounds and the people setting up for the day, they stopped walking.

"So what do we do now?" Cooper asked.

"I don't know," Gelfroy said. "Why did you two come down here in the first place?"

"We just wanted to know what was down here," Priscilla said. "Why Aeris came down, where I came from. I just wanted answers."

"Well, we can't have you leading the hunt down here," Gelfroy said. "It could be disastrous."

"I hate to say this, Pris," Cooper sighed. "But you have to go back."

"But I just found you," Priscilla objected. "I don't want to go back."

"If you stay, you'll bring the Hunt down here to them," Dothar said. "To the innocents here. You can't do that to them. We must go back before we become the hunted ourselves."

"It's too late for that," a voice said from the trees behind them.

They all turned to see a centaur emerging from the pine trees. A small group of other creatures from the Hunt were following close behind him.

"Kezzryn," Dothar turned to the centaur. "Why have you come down here?"

"We came to see why our Queen has run off," the centaur said.

"I haven't run off," Priscilla said, stepping in front of Dothar. "We were scouting down the mountain."

"Just like Aeris went scouting and found you?" Kezzryn said. "It looks like you got twice as lucky as he did."

The centaur eyed Gelfroy and Cooper.

The two young men were speechless, staring at the half-man half-horse creature in front of them.

"A surety for each of you?" the centaur looked back to Priscilla.

"They are not a surety," Priscilla said. "Only I can grant one permission for a surety, and we don't need any."

"You don't have any authority over me at this moment," Kezzryn said.

"I am your Queen," Priscilla stood as tall as her short stature would allow. "You forget yourself, centaur. I decide who needs a surety, and I decide who is in a scouting party. As well as the fact that I decide when a member of the Hunt has left the grounds without permission, as you and your friends have."

"I have never known a leader of the Hunt to be a scout," Kezzryn said. "They usually send someone else to do that. So, the only conclusion I can come to is that you were trying to escape."

"Yes, and when someone tried to escape, they head home when they are done," Dothar said in a mocking tone.

"Don't mock me, you human weakling," the centaur said.

"I will mock you until the day I kill you," Dothar said with a smirk. "At least I'm not a horse's ass."

"I have waited a long time to hunt the likes of you," the centaur growled. "And taking over from the Ice Queen, that will just be icing on the cake."

"Be quiet," Priscilla commanded.

The centaur stared at the Ice Queen.

Priscilla stepped towards the centaur and faced off with him, "We will all head back up the mountain and settle this on the battlegrounds."

"A challenge then," Kezzryn said. "I accept. Make sure you bring your sureties with you, or the Hunt will continue with your little town as its new hunting grounds."

The centaur and his followers turned and stormed off up the mountain.

"We can't let them come down the mountain," Gelfroy said.

Priscilla looked down the way they had come from the faire grounds. She then looked at Gelfroy and Cooper sadly.

"We will go to the battlegrounds with you," Cooper said.

"You will never come back," she said to them.

The two men looked behind them and then back to Priscilla.

"It doesn't matter," Gelfroy said. "We have to protect everyone down here from the Hunt encroaching any further than it already has."

Priscilla nodded grimly, "You two are very brave."

"Or very stupid," Dothar said.

"Don't mock them as well," Priscilla said. "They are giving their lives freely to protect others."

"Yeah, brave, stupid, it can go either way," Cooper said.

"I'm opting for brave," Gelfroy said. "I've never done a brave thing in my life, so it's about time I did."

Gelfroy led the way up the mountain with the others falling in behind him.

As they got farther up the mountain, Gelfroy and Cooper gasped for air as it thinned with the altitude.

The small party stopped to let the two humans rest for a few moments.

"Are you still feeling brave now?" Cooper asked Gelfroy.

"Shut up," Gelfroy gasped. "And yes."

*

As they approached the battlegrounds, Gelfroy and Cooper followed behind Priscilla and Dothar. Gelfroy was wrapped in Priscilla's woolen cape, and Cooper was wearing Dothar's. The two men shivered from the cold in the snow and the darkness.

Priscilla and Dothar entered the center of the crowd of creatures that had been gathering for the upcoming battle. Gelfroy and Cooper followed closely behind them.

Kezzryn met them in the middle of the makeshift arena.

"I formally challenge the Ice Queen to a battle to the death, for her title as Master of the Hunt," Kezzryn announced.

The creatures in the circle cheered loudly. Some chanting for the centaur, some for the Ice Queen.

Dothar stepped forward, "I will be the champion for the Ice Queen."

"No," Kezzryn said. "I do not accept a champion."

The crowd went silent.

It was not usual for a champion to be turned down.

"I challenge the Ice Queen," Kezzryn said. "I allege that she is not fit to lead us, and a champion fighting in her place will not give a satisfactory determination of that allegation."

The crowd of creatures erupted in a cheer of agreement.

"You cannot turn down a champion," Dothar yelled.

"Yes, I can," Kezzryn said. "I am challenging her ability to lead."

"I will fight him," Priscilla said.

"No, my Queen," Dothar said.

"If she wants to save the lives of these two," the centaur gestured to Gelfroy and Cooper. "She will face me herself."

The crowd went silent once more. Even the snarling hellhounds went silent as Priscilla stepped up to face the centaur.

"We will fight to the death," Priscilla said. "And when I win, no one will challenge my leadership again."

"No one can make that promise," Kezzryn laughed.

Priscilla stared the centaur straight in the eyes, "I can."

The crowd cheered in agreement once again.

Kezzryn snorted, "Agreed."

Dothar stepped back, guiding Gelfroy and Cooper out of the way of the impending battle.

Kezzryn stepped sideways, in an attempt to circle Priscilla. She held her ax at the ready.

The centaur pulled a sword from a sheath at his side and charged at Priscilla full speed.

Priscilla blocked the attack with her ax, but the blow from the sword cut the ax handle in half, leaving Priscilla with just a fragment of splintered wood in her hands.

The crowd roared with approval. Other centaurs started to chant Kezzryn's name. The night elves roared loudly for the Ice Queen.

Cooper and Gelfroy stood by helplessly as they watched Priscilla turn to face Kezzryn as he circled back around for another go at her with his sword.

Dothar unsheathed his sword and stood ready to toss it to Priscilla. But she never looked his way.

Instead, the Ice Queen faced the centaur, her eyes locked on him as he charged towards her. Kezzryn raised his sword to strike the unarmed Ice Queen.

Priscilla raised her arms and threw her head back. An icy wind whipped up out of nowhere and Kezzryn stopped dead right in front of her with his sword poised for a killing blow. The centaur was frozen solid, like an ice sculpture, with the Ice Queen standing calmly, looking at him as if admiring her own artwork.

The crowd of creatures went into a stunned silence and stared at the Queen, who was now circling the frozen centaur, dragging her index finger along him as she went. When she circled back to the front of the frozen statue of Kezzryn, she pushed gently and the top half of the ice figure slid off and shattered into thousands of pieces on the ground, leaving just the bottom half of the horse figure standing in front of her.

With the crowd still in a stunned silence, Priscilla turned to the crowd and said, "Now that I have won, no one will challenge my leadership again."

The creatures in the crowd roared in agreement and started to chant "Ice Queen" over and over.

Priscilla looked over at her friends and saw them staring at her with a look of shock on their faces, Dothar included.

She walked over to them as the crowd of creatures ran into the center of the battle circle to touch the remains of Kezzryn.

"I can't believe you did that," Gelfroy said in amazement.

"I can't believe I've been fighting your battles all this time," Dothar said.

"That was so cool!" Cooper said.

"I can't change the rules, you know," Priscilla looked at Cooper and Gelfroy.

"What do you mean?" Gelfroy asked.

"You've seen the Wild Hunt," she said sadly. "You must join or die."

"You can't send us home?' Gelfroy asked.

"No," she shook her head sadly. "I have no control over those rules."

"If I join," Cooper asked. "Do I get cool armor like Dothar?"

"You get the armor that suits you," Dothar nodded.

"Will you train me?" Cooper asked.

Dothar looked at Priscilla, who gave the slightest nod.

"She doesn't need me enough for me to neglect an apprentice," Dothar said.

"Yes," Cooper said with excitement.

"This means we can't go home," Gelfroy said. "We'll forget our memories. Just like Priscilla and Aeris."

"Our memories?" Cooper looked back over at Gelfroy. "We get to be fighters!"

"It's already happening," Priscilla said to Gelfroy.

They watched as Cooper walked off with Dothar. Cooper was already wearing shiny new armor and was swinging a sword that he unsheathed from his side.

"I can't kill," Gelfroy looked at Priscilla, and absently raised his hood over his head.

"Look at you," Priscilla said. "You're a friar. No one will expect you to kill."

"But won't that get me killed?" he asked. "Don't the weak get hunted?"

Priscilla shook her head, "No, you will be my consult."

"What do you mean?" Gelfroy asked.

"You will stay at my side and no one will challenge you," she answered. "And you will be my voice of conscience. My guide."

"Does the Wild Hunt have room for a conscience?" he asked.

"It will as long as I reign," Priscilla answered.

More books by Judy Lunsford:

Gamers
Schemers

Fire Lily
Bezbell
Kirog

Moonlight Magic
Moonlight Melody

The Red Dart
Shadow Mountain

The Portal Wars
The Grimoires

Short Story Collections:
The Dark of Night
Fairy Short Stories
Fairy Tales & Nightmares
Fantasy Faire
Fae Reigns
First Stories
Magic from the Dark
Story Hoard
The Wild Hunt

Thank you for reading.
If you enjoyed this book, you can find more stories
at
JudyLunsford.com
or your favorite online retailer.

www.ingramcontent.com/pod-product-compliance
Lightning Source LLC
Chambersburg PA
CBHW061518120726

48001CB00004B/1356